INSIDE MY HEAD

JIM CARRINGTON

LONDON BERLIN NEW YORK SYDNEY

Bloomsbury Publishing, London, Berlin and New York

First published in Great Britain in April 2010 by Bloomsbury Publishing Plc
36 Soho Square, London, W1D 3QY

A CIP catalogue record of this book is available from the British Library

ISBN 978 1 4088 0271 7

Typeset by Dorchester Typesetting Group Ltd
Printed in Great Britain by Clays Ltd, St Ives plc, Bungay, Suffolk

3 5 7 9 10 8 6 4

www.bloomsbury.com/childrens

INSIDE MY HEAD

For my family

PART ONE

THURSDAY

Zoë

The house is a complete mess. There are boxes with Dad's handwriting on them everywhere: *lounge*, *dining room*, *kitchen*, blah-blah-blah. I have to step round them to get into the kitchen.

'Morning, love,' Mum says, standing in front of the sink stroking her massive pregnant belly. The sun floods in through the window behind her. Dad's sitting at the table, fiddling about with a screwdriver and the plug on a lamp. He doesn't even look up at me.

I kind of mumble a reply. I'm not awake enough for proper words just yet.

'Bit of unpacking today, Zoë. Yeah?' Mum says. 'Get this place sorted out, get it looking like a home! Our new home in the country.' She smiles. She's way too enthusiastic.

So I don't answer her. I open kitchen cupboards instead. They're all empty. No bowls. No cereal. Nothing.

'What you looking for, love?' Mum says.

'Cornflakes.'

'Over here. On the floor,' Dad says. 'In this packing box.'

I walk over, grab the cornflakes. 'Where's the bowls?'

'In the hallway,' Dad says. 'There's an open box marked *kitchen*. Spoons are in there as well.'

I sigh, put the cornflakes on the table and walk through to the hall, grab a spoon and a bowl and stomp back to the table.

'Sleep well, love?' Mum asks.

I don't answer. I didn't sleep well. I was thinking about everything that I'm missing in London.

'It's so much quieter at night here than back in London,' Mum says.

I pour cornflakes into my bowl and grab the milk bottle.

'It gets darker at night as well,' Mum says. 'There's less light pollution. Have a look up at the sky tonight, Zoë. It'll be full of stars.'

I don't say anything. I just shovel spoonfuls of cornflakes into my mouth and wish that I was anywhere else but here.

David

Right now, I'm on my stool in Mr Hambleton's lesson, in his manky science lab that stinks of gas and chemicals and burnt splints. Mr H has just shown us an experiment – some chemical reaction or other – but because I was too busy messing about with Knaggs and Joe and Mills, I have no idea what happened. We're supposed to be writing the experiment up in our books now, answering some questions and all that stuff. My exercise book is open, but I haven't written a thing. And sitting next to me, to my right, is Knaggs. His book's still closed. He's playing with the gas tap in the middle of the bench, pretending to switch it on and off.

'Wouldn't it be cool to just switch the gas on?' he says. He turns to me with a smile on his face. 'Just let the lab fill up with gas!'

I shrug my shoulders. 'Yeah, s'pose. Be dangerous, though, wouldn't it, inhaling all that gas?'

'No. It'd be all right,' Knaggs says, fiddling with the tap again. 'You'd only inhale a bit, cos we'd tell Mr H and he'd have to evacuate us, wouldn't he? We'd get the rest of the day off school! Think about it.'

I smile. The rest of the day off school would be great.

Joe, who's sitting opposite me and Knaggs, looks up at us. 'Imagine how much trouble you'd get in, Knaggs,' he says. 'They'd chuck you out for good if you did something like that.'

Knaggs shrugs. 'They wouldn't know who'd done it,' he says. 'Not unless some little puddleface grassed me up.'

'I'm not saying anyone'd grass on you,' Joe says. 'I was thinking what if they could tell which tap the gas had come out of?'

Knaggs makes a face, like he couldn't care less. He laughs. 'Yeah, right. Like they have sensors on the gas taps! Or CCTV. Get real, Joe.'

I laugh too. I can tell today's is gonna be one of those lessons. In half an hour I'm gonna come out of the lab with that weird guilty feeling, like I've got away with something I shouldn't have. I can feel it in the air. Things are gonna get silly. They always do in Mr Hambleton's lessons. 'So are you gonna do it, then, Knaggs? You gonna switch the gas on?' I say.

Knaggs smiles. 'Yeah. Watch this,' he says. And he opens the gas tap. Only when he does, absolutely nothing happens.

Mills looks up from his book. From the look of it, he's nearly finished his write-up already. 'It's switched off at the mains, you pebblehead,' he says in this kind of tired, bored-sounding voice. 'Do you really think they'd trust us to have the gas taps on all the time?'

Knaggs closes the gas tap. He looks up. He sort of looks embarrassed for a second. But then he smiles. 'Course I knew it was switched off at the mains,' he says. 'I was just shitting you all up. You should have seen your faces. Pebbleheads!'

It goes quiet on our bench for a while. No one wants to say anything. After a bit, I decide I might as well get some work done, so I pick up my fountain pen and start writing: date, title, sub-heading, blah-blah-blah. I get quite a lot done, even up to the method and the diagram and the results table. But then I get a nudge from over to my right. Knaggs again. He knocks my arm so that I end up drawing on my own work.

'Knaggs, you plum,' I say. 'Look what you've done.'

But Knaggs ignores what I say and points to the

front of the class. Gary Wood has come in late. He's talking to Mr Hambleton, although I can't hear what he's saying cos it's so noisy in the lab.

'Farmer Boy's late again,' Knaggs says. 'I reckon his dad's tractor must've broken down!'

I laugh. See, at our school, being a farmer is bad news and calling someone a farmer is like a term of abuse.

I watch Mr H tell Wood what to do for a few seconds. But halfway through, Mr H stops talking and looks up at the classroom. 'Year Ten, keep the noise down, please,' he says. 'You've only got twenty minutes till the end of the lesson. I want you all finished! Otherwise you'll stay in at break.'

He's right about the noise and the amount of time till the end of the lesson. But everyone knows that he doesn't mean what he says about staying in at break-time. Mr Hambleton always threatens to keep people in at break if they don't finish, but everyone knows that what he'll actually do is keep you in for about a minute before he realises that he wants to get out of the lab and he'll just let you go. Happens every time. And you know why? Cos Mr H is a smoker and he wants to get to the school gate so he can have a fag. It's true.

Most people are looking at their books now. It's a bit quieter in the lab. Won't last long, though – it never does. I get back to my work too, start to put the results in the table. Beside me I can sense that Knaggs still isn't getting on with his work, though. He's messing about with the gas tap again, staring into space. His book is shut.

'You could do it,' Knaggs says suddenly. 'All you'd have to do is find the mains gas tap and turn that on at the start of the lesson. It's probably in the prep room, isn't it? Then all the taps in the lab'd be on, wouldn't they?'

I don't look up. I finish putting numbers in the results table.

But Mills is nearly finished. He puts his pen down. 'They'd catch you, Knaggs,' he says. 'They'd find your fingerprints on the taps, you plum.'

I laugh. I put my pen down and look up.

Knaggs doesn't laugh, though, he just smiles. 'Wrong!' he says. 'I'd wear gloves, Mills, you puddle-face!' And he gives Mills the middle finger.

We all laugh.

Over to my right, I can see Wood sitting down. He doesn't talk to anyone, just opens his book and gets writing.

'So,' says Mills, 'you're gonna wear gloves when you set off the gas taps, yeah? That's decided, is it?'

'Yeah,' says Knaggs, smiling. 'Course. The perfect crime.'

'Brilliant,' says Mills. He laughs. He's a sarcastic bugger, Mills. 'So, then all the cops'd have to do is find the idiot wearing gloves in the science lesson and they'd've got the culprit! Told you, you're a plum.'

We all laugh.

Mr H looks up again. 'Quieten down,' he says. 'Fifteen minutes till the bell now. You must get finished.'

So I look at my book again. I'm getting to the difficult bit now. I'm s'posed to write a conclusion from the results and then answer some questions from a textbook. And seeing as I have no idea what the experiment was really about, I might have to borrow Mills's book to see what I'm meant to write. I look around for something to distract me, so I won't have to try and figure out what the investigation was s'posed to show for a while. But all around me, people have their heads down, writing. And Mr H has started prowling round the classroom, looking over shoulders at people's work. So I get my head down too, look at the results, try and work out what the hell they mean. But it's no use. I could sit here and stare at them for the rest of my life and I still wouldn't have a clue. So I look up, check whether Mr H is watching, and then lean across and tap Mills on the arm.

'What?'

'What have you written in your conclusion?'

Mills looks around, sees that Mr H is standing on the other side of the lab, behind Rachel Cluck, and passes his book across the bench. I grab it and start writing, change the odd word here and there so it doesn't look too obvious that I've cheated. Knaggs does the same. He's managed to catch up with me somehow.

It's quiet in the lab for a little while. Don't know why. Certainly wasn't cos of anything Mr H said. Maybe it's cos he's walking round the class, checking on people's work. He's getting close to our bench now. I finish copying down Mills's conclusion and push the book back to the other side of the bench. And about thirty seconds later, Mr H comes walking past our bench, looking over our shoulders.

'OK, boys,' he says. 'Make sure you get the questions done as well.'

As soon as he's gone, me, Knaggs, Mills and Joe laugh. And we all stop writing. Knaggs leans over to his right to talk to Wood, who's at the other end of the bench. 'Hey, Farmer Boy,' he says. 'I see you were late this morning.'

Wood looks up at him, but doesn't say anything.

'What's the problem? Tractor break down or something?'

I laugh. So does Knaggs.

But Wood just looks straight back at Knaggs. He

isn't smiling. 'Shut up,' he says. He bends over his book again and starts to write.

Knaggs leans back to our part of the bench. 'Hey, lads,' he says. 'Do you know this one?' And then he puts on this fake Norfolk accent:

'Oi carn't read,

oi carn't write,

but that don't really matter.

Cos my name is Gary Wood

and I can drive a tractor!'

That's funny. We all have a laugh at that. I look at Wood. He's still writing, trying to pretend he isn't annoyed. But you can tell he is. He's staring way too hard at his work. He'll burn a hole in it if he isn't careful.

I look at my watch. Still another five minutes or so till the bell. I think about starting on the questions in the textbook. But over to my right I can see Knaggs leaning towards Wood again. This'll be funny. I'll do the questions in a bit.

'Hey, Wood,' Knaggs says.

'Leave me alone.' Wood doesn't even look up.

'What's it like being so ugly?' Knaggs says.

Wood doesn't reply, but the rest of us on the bench snigger. Knaggs does this a lot and it's funny as hell.

'Just asking,' Knaggs says. 'You know, I used to

think that you must be the ugliest person on the planet, Gary.'

Wood isn't writing any more. He's gripping his pen tightly, just staring at his book.

'Well, that's what I used to think,' Knaggs goes on.

I let out a little laugh, cos I already know the punchline.

'That is, till I saw your mum on the internet. Man, is she ugly!'

Everyone on the bench bursts out laughing. It's so loud that Mr H looks round at our bench and we all hush up a bit.

I look at Wood for a reaction. He bristles a bit. But then he sort of sits upright, puffs himself out, like words can't hurt him. He looks over at Knaggs. 'Yeah, well, I'd rather be ugly than a short-arse,' he says.

No one laughs at that. There are just a load of faces that say *'That's not funny'*. And Wood looks embarrassed that he said it. Wood's face has gone red. I can see a vein sticking out on his temple. He looks like he's gonna burst a blood vessel.

Maybe Knaggs should give it a rest now. But he doesn't. He leans across again.

'Is it true your mum and dad met in a factory?' Knaggs says to Wood.

Wood puts his pen down and shuts his book. He stares at the bench. His eyes are bulging. He's so angry it's difficult to look at him.

'I heard they were just two lonely cheese puffs, travelling along the conveyor belt, when their eyes met. Love at first sight.'

Wood looks up. He takes a deep breath. His jaw's clenched. 'Shut the fuck up, Knaggs,' he says, quiet.

'What?' says Knaggs, smiling, pretending to be all innocent. 'I thought it was a nice story. And, you know, it explains why you look so much like a delicious cheesy corn snack!'

Everyone laughs again. See, the funny thing about Wood – apart from the fact that he's a farmer – is that his head looks exactly like a cheese puff. Seriously! It does. His face is covered in big orange freckles and his hair's all short and ginger. Even his eyelashes look like they're covered in cheese-puff dust. It would be tragic if it wasn't so funny.

But Wood's not laughing. He looks like he's trying not to explode. 'Shut your face, or I'll fucking kill you,' he says to Knaggs.

Knaggs just laughs. 'No need to be so aggressive, Gary,' he says.

'There are a couple of minutes to the bell,' Mr H calls out over the noise that's built up in the lab again. 'You must have answered at least the first three questions before you leave this room.'

So we all kind of quieten down again, look back at

our books. I try and answer the first three questions. If I at least get something written for them, I'll be able to go when the bell goes. But soon I feel a nudge in my ribs. Knaggs. He points over to Wood. Wood is just sitting there, staring at the bench, jaw clenched, eyes bulging. Knaggs smiles at me. I've got that weird guilty feeling already.

Zoë

My new room sucks. It has four blue walls with nothing on them except little greasy patches where someone else stuck their pictures up with Blu-tack. It has a crappy little window with a view out over the crappy little garden. There's a cracked patio out there, some grass and a wonky shed. The only furniture in my room is my bed, desk and wardrobe. They look wrong here, in this room. They should be in the flat in Morden. So should I. Right in the middle of the floor there's a pile of taped-up boxes, with Dad's handwriting on them: *Zoë's room*. They're not opened yet. Cos I can't do it. Cos as soon as I take all my stuff out and put it in this room, it's like saying that this is *my* new room, that I'm here to stay. And I don't want to even think about that.

Course, I didn't get a say where we moved. Not really. Mum asked me what I thought about it. And I said I didn't want to move. I said I already had a home and a school. In Morden. And so here we are, in Norfolk, the arse end of nowhere. The land that time forgot. Where brothers and sisters get married. That's what Rianna said. Her cousin lives near Norwich. She reckons most people in Norfolk have webbed fingers!

And all of this is so Mum and Dad's little baby can grow up in the countryside and not turn into a messed-up teenager like me. So it can't get led astray, like they think I've been. Cos the thing about Mum and Dad is they don't trust me to live my own life the way that *I* want to live it. They think I'm a sheep. Like, for instance, I have this friend Jodie who cuts herself, or at least she did a while back. So Mum put two and two together, came up with five and figured that I must be doing it as well. Like I don't have a brain of my own, like I can't think for myself. And one day I had a scratch on my arm from getting a ball out of the hedge in PE and Mum went absolutely mental. Even when I explained to her, when I swore on my life that it had happened in PE, she didn't know whether to believe me or not.

I get up off the floor and walk over to the window.

How can they even call that a garden? When Mum said that we'd have a house in the countryside with a garden, I thought it'd have a thatched roof and roses. But the reality is the ugliest house you've ever seen. It's like the kind of house a little kid makes out of Lego. Only much worse.

It's doing my head in. This room. This house. Mum. Dad. The baby. Everything. There's only one thing for it. I head down the stairs to our new tacky white plastic front door and I open it.

And just as I'm closing the door behind me, I yell out, 'I'm going out.'

And I'm gone before anyone can stop me.

David

I'm already on question four as the bell goes.

'Hand in your books when you've finished,' Mr H calls over the noise. 'Then you can leave.'

Mills and me hand our books in and walk out of the lab, to the cloakroom.

About thirty seconds later, Knaggs joins us. 'D'you see Wood?' he says. 'I thought he was gonna start blubbing!'

I nod my head. 'Yeah, I know,' I say. 'He looked like he was gonna explode.'

'Leave it now, though,' Mills says. 'You know what he's like.'

I nod.

Knaggs shrugs. 'He won't do anything. He's a pussy!'

No one answers him. I avoid Knaggs's eyes.

We all set about looking for our blazers and bags on the floor of the cloakroom. I find my blazer, brush the dust off it and start looking for my bag.

Then there's a noise. *SMACK!* Loud and shocking.

The whole place goes silent and we all turn to look. Knaggs is lying on the floor of the cloakroom, holding the side of his face. His mouth is open. He looks stunned. For a second, I'm confused. But then my brain starts to fill in the missing parts and I look around for Wood. But he's not there. The door out of the cloakroom swings shut.

We all crowd round Knaggs.

Mr Moore comes and gets me out of literacy, next lesson. He doesn't say what it's about. He just walks me through the empty corridors in silence. But it's obvious what he wants me for.

When we get to his office, I expect to see Knaggs sitting there. But he isn't. Neither's Wood.

'Take a seat, David,' Mr Moore says. He points at a comfy green chair.

I sit down in it and sink back. But I feel awkward, so I sit up straight instead. My hands are sweaty. My heart's pounding.

Mr Moore starts off, going on about how I'm a responsible boy and that he trusts me to tell the truth and all that stuff. I just sit there feeling weird. See, I know what he's gonna ask me to do. He wants me to point the finger. He wants me to grass someone up. Knaggs or Wood. It's what teachers always want – some mug like me to make their job easier. I have a decision to make, I know. I can tell him the truth and keep the teachers' rules. But the thing is, then I'd be breaking the kid rules. I'd be breaking the biggest kid rule of all: grassing up my best mate. Or I can lie. It's the kind of choice where I have no choice.

'Tell me what happened in the science lab, David,' Mr Moore says.

I sit and think for a moment. The truth's easy. I know exactly what happened. We were messing about all lesson, like normal, and Knaggs started taking the mick out of Wood. The rest of us just encouraged him to do it. But Knaggs pushed it too far. Anyone could see how angry Wood was getting – he was about to explode. And then Wood went mental. But I can't say any of that, not the stuff that actually happened. Knaggs would get into trouble. I'm gonna have to lie, bend the truth a little. Otherwise my life won't be worth living. I shift uncomfortably in my seat. I've got a nervous guilty feeling in my stomach and I haven't even started lying yet.

'Was there an argument, David?' Mr Moore says. 'Tell me what you remember . . .'

I look up at him. He's looking straight at me, almost smiling but not quite. I take a deep breath. 'It started when Gary came into science late, sir,' I say. No lies yet but my heart's still beating like crazy. 'Gary and Knaggs – I mean, Paul Knaggs – well, they were having a laugh, taking the mickey out of each other, just winding each other up.' My voice is shaking slightly. It doesn't sound like me talking.

Mr Moore picks a notebook up off his desk and then a pen. He writes something down. And then he stops and looks up at me again. He smiles. 'It was both of them, you say?'

I nod.

Mr Moore makes more notes. Then he looks up at me. 'OK. How were they winding each other up, David?'

I look down at my feet. 'Don't know. Just the usual, really. They always do it. Just calling each other names and that. It was nothing serious, sir. It was just a bit of give and take.'

I look up. Mr Moore's writing more things in his notebook and nodding his head. Over his shoulder I can see a signed cricket bat and an old photo of the school team. I stare at them. God, I wish I was outside playing cricket instead of sitting here.

'Go on,' Mr Moore says.

I look back at him with a start. I must look guilty as hell. So I look at my shoes again. See, I'm a rubbish liar. People can see it in my eyes straight away. I can't hide it. 'Well, then we all got on with our work. Tried to get it all finished before the end of the lesson. Except Gary. He just sort of sat there and stared at the desk. He looked angry. And then he tried to start it all up again,' I say. And I hate myself for saying it. I think of Wood sitting there in the lab, with that angry face, taking it all. I should be telling Mr Moore about that. But I can't. I can't grass on Knaggs. That's the rules. The kid rules. He's my mate. I have to stick up for him. 'Gary kept trying to start it all off again, calling Paul short and that. And so Paul took the mickey back a bit. And that's when Gary started to look *really* angry, like he couldn't handle it any more.'

Mr Moore raises his eyebrows. 'I see,' he says. 'Can you remember exactly what was said?'

I stare back at him. The 'sort of' smile has gone from his face. He looks serious now. I feel like he's about to rumble me. I shake my head. 'Not exactly, sir,' I say. I look up at the cricket bat again, to avoid looking in his eyes. 'Gary was taking the mickey out of Paul for being short. And Paul was taking the mickey back, saying Gary's head looks like a cheese puff. And then Gary just got really angry. He said he was gonna kill Paul – that sort of stuff.'

Mr Moore raises his eyebrows again and notes something else down in his book. He underlines it three times, then looks back at me. 'You're sure that's what he said, David . . . ?'

I nod. 'Yeah.' My heart's thumping so hard I can hear it in my ears. I feel sick. I want to be out of this room.

'Absolutely sure . . . ?'

I take a breath. 'Yes.'

'Thank you, David,' Mr Moore says. And then he shows me to the door.

Zoë

There's not much in this village. But there is a shop. When we came here to look a few months back – when Mum found out she was having a baby and decided we had to get out of London – she bought me an ice cream and took me to the park, like I was a little kid.

The shop's about five minutes' walk away, on the village green. I have to walk on the road, cos they don't seem to have heard of pavements in the countryside. There's just a grass verge that's soaking wet. When I get near the shop, I check my purse: 31p. I look both ways. No traffic. So I cross.

There's a sign on the door in neat handwriting:

Only two schoolchildren are permitted to enter the shop at any one time. It makes me think of Morden. There's a shop near my school. My old school. There's a sign there as well. Not quite as neat, though. Or as polite. It got put up after Jodie started stealing sweets and giving them away. That was back in year seven. She doesn't do that any more.

Inside it's tiny, like a corridor with shelves on either side. Everything looks old and shabby, like a museum. The sweets are near the counter, at the end of the corridor. Behind the counter there's an old lady, wearing one of those old-lady aprons, the ones that are more like coats. As I take a look at the rack of sweets I can see her out of the corner of my eye, staring at me down her nose. She's probably looking at me in my black hoodie. I know what she's thinking: Teenager + Black Hoodie = Shoplifter. I ignore her, concentrate on the chocolate. There isn't much to choose from here: Mars, Snickers, Twix, KitKat, Turkish Delight, Bounty Dark and Chomp. Every single bar has a price sticker on it. 31p isn't enough for anything except a Chomp bar. I pick one off the shelf and hand it to the old lady. She smiles as she takes it.

'Not at school today, dear?'

My stomach turns over. I look up at her. She's still smiling. I shake my head. 'Haven't started yet,' I say. 'We just moved here yesterday.'

'Oh, how lovely,' she says. Then she picks up the bar code scanner. She holds it like it might bite her. She waves the Chomp bar in front of it until there's a beep. 'Fifteen pence, please, dear,' she says.

I hand her the money and she hands me the chocolate.

'Thanks,' I say.

She smiles again. 'You'll like it round here,' she says. 'There are lots of nice young people in the village, lots of things to do.'

I smile at her, put the chocolate in the front pocket of my hoodie and then leave the shop.

David

We're all in the playground, with our backs against the chain-link fence, eating our sandwiches. All except Knaggs. He's been in with Mr Moore for ages. Hope I didn't say anything by mistake that's got him in trouble. Don't think I did. Probably Wood has grassed on him. I mean, what's Wood got to lose? He's pretty much the lowest of the low anyway. He has no friends, so it's not like he can lose any. And most people are too scared of him to try and fight him, cos of the way he loses his temper. Or maybe Mr Moore saw through the lies that I was telling him. Even teachers can tell when people are lying, surely. Sometimes. I mean, Mr Moore must know that there are kid rules, that

I wasn't gonna grass on Knaggs, that he's my mate. He'll probably call me back in, give me a bollocking for lying.

But as I'm eating my cheese sandwiches, the double door out to the playground swings open and Knaggs walks out. He swaggers over towards us. He looks pretty happy with himself for someone who's been smacked in the gob. I guess he can't have got into trouble after all. I get up and walk towards him. Joe and Mills follow.

'What happened? You in trouble?' I say.

Knaggs grins. 'You won't believe this,' he says. 'This is so funny.' He pauses.

We stare back at him, eager to hear.

'I didn't get in trouble at all!' he says. 'Mr Moore made Wood apologise to me!'

We laugh. 'Seriously?'

'Yeah,' Knaggs says. 'Wood's in *so* much trouble. Mr Moore said it was cos of what you said to him, Davey-boy.' Knaggs looks straight at me and smiles. 'Nice one. You're my star witness!'

I smile. Then I look away. In my head I can picture Wood sitting in the science lab, his eyes bulging, the veins in his temples pulsing.

'What did you say to Mr Moore?' Mills says. 'How did you manage to get Knaggs off the hook? He was as guilty as a dog with a string of sausages hanging out of its mouth.'

I shrug. 'Just said that Wood went a bit over the top, that's all,' I say.

Mills laughs and spins round on his heels. 'Well, whatever you said, you should be a defence lawyer. You'd earn millions if you can get a man as guilty as Knaggs out of trouble!'

'Shut up, Mills,' says Knaggs. 'Anyway, I haven't got to the best bit yet. I had to wait in the office while Wood's mum came and picked him up. He's been excluded till next week! And they're gonna try and get him sent to a shrink! I swear he was crying.'

We laugh again. But I don't laugh very hard or very long. It doesn't feel right.

'Why are they doing that?' I say.

Knaggs looks like he thinks this is the funniest thing that's ever happened in the history of the world. 'Well, duh,' he says. 'Maybe it's because he's a complete frigging psycho! I'm not the first person he's hit for no reason, Davey-boy. He hit a year seven kid the other day!'

I should say something. Someone should. Why doesn't Mills tell Knaggs he's being a div? Why doesn't he tell him that he wasn't hit for no reason? Why don't I tell him?

Kid rules, that's why. Standing by your mates is more important than knowing what's the right thing to do.

I walk back over to the fence and sit down. I close my lunch box. I'm not all that hungry any more.

Gary

As soon as we get to the house, I can hear Patch barking from the back garden. Poor sod gets left out there every day. Mum and me walk up the path to the house. I stand on the step as Mum tries to open the front door – Dad still hasn't mended it. Mum turns the key and then forces the door with her shoulder and her foot. It needs planing and sanding down, cos it sticks whenever it's damp outside. Mum's been at Dad to do it for ages. She might as well save her breath.

Mum wipes her feet on the mat. She holds the door open for me, staring at me, silent. She's got this look on her face. I don't know what it means. She looks fed up with me, though. Ashamed, most likely.

'Wipe your feet, Gary,' she says as I walk in.

I shuffle my feet on the mat.

'Now, Gary, I want you to go upstairs and get changed out of your school uniform,' she says. 'And while you're up there, you can have a think about what you've done, young man. Do you understand me?'

I nod.

'I'll come and get you when your lunch is ready.' She turns and walks towards the kitchen.

I stomp up the stairs slowly, imagining each one is Paul Knaggs's ugly fucker little head. By the time I get to the landing I'm sobbing. No tears, only sobs that sound like geese honking. I sink to my knees, bury my head in my hands and just kneel there, in a little ball outside my room. I can hear Mum downstairs, in the kitchen. She's put the radio on. Bloody country and western music. She's banging around in the cupboards, getting plates out and stuff. And all the while I kneel there, thinking about Paul Fucking Knaggs. He'll be with his smug friends at school, taking the mickey out of me. I saw him waiting outside Mr Moore's office when Mum took me home. He was smiling. Bastard. I wish I'd killed him. Moore would have to kick me out for good then. I'd never have to go back to Wendham High School.

I'm grinding my teeth – I can feel it. But I can't stop

it. My jaw aches like mad. Feels like every muscle in my body is twitching, angry, tense. My fingers ball up into fists. I want to hit something, I want to hit someone. I want to hit Paul Knaggs, knock that smug grin off his face for good. But I punch the carpet instead – one, two, three, four times. And then I stand up. I can feel real tears now, running down my face. They're hot, feel like they're burning my face. I open my bedroom door, go in and slam it behind me. My shitty cheapo trainers are on the floor right in front of me. I take a swing at one of them, kick it. It flies up and across the room, hits the window and then falls to the carpet. It leaves a mess of dried mud on the carpet. I look at the other trainer lying there, and I kick that as well. It skids across the floor, hits the wall and leaves another mess.

I feel like hitting something else. Smashing it to pieces. But there ain't anything else around, apart from my clothes. So I take a deep breath. And another. And another. Try and calm down. I get on to my bed and sigh. I start thinking. My brain starts rushing. A million things rush through it. Who the fuck does Knaggs think he is? He don't know anything about me. All that shit about cheese puffs and farmers. He makes me so bloody angry, acting like everything about him is good and everything about me is shit. Well, maybe he's right.

I close my eyes, put my head in my hands and sigh. The tears have dried on my cheeks now – I can feel little dried-up bits of salt where they ran. I just sit here, on my bed – head in my hands, eyes closed – and I do nothing. I can't even think straight. I sit and make a kind of growling noise. Don't know where it comes from. My jaw clenches up. It feels like there's a balloon inside my head, filling up with air, squashing the insides of my skull. It feels like it's gonna explode, cover the room in little bits of my stupid ginger cheese-puff brain.

I hear Mum clomping up the stairs. And I don't want her to see me like this. I take my head out of my hands and stare in front of me at nothing. Mum knocks twice on my door. She opens it and stands there in the doorway. She has her hands on her hips. She's looking straight at me, I can tell, but I don't look back at her. I can't. I'll cry or something.

'I thought I told you to get changed out of your uniform,' she says.

I don't say anything. I just stare in front of me, like she ain't there.

She tuts, then says, 'Come on, Gary. Your lunch is ready.'

I don't say anything, don't look at her. And after five seconds of standing there staring at me, she tuts again, turns and goes back downstairs.

I clench my fists and close my eyes. I can feel a sob

coming on. But I screw my face up and ride it out. And after a minute, I get off the bed and follow her downstairs.

Mum's sitting at the table in the kitchen with a cup of tea in her hands. Patch is sitting on the kitchen floor, at Mum's feet. He wags his tail when I come into the room. Mum looks up at me. She gets up, goes over to the sideboard and comes back with a plate. There's a cheese sandwich on it. And next to the sandwich, there's a pile of cheese puffs. I'm not hungry.

'Here you go,' she says. 'Sit down. Eat this and you might feel a bit better.'

I sit down and stare at it. It makes me feel sick. She might as well have served up a dog shit on a plate. I'm not eating anything.

'Do you want a drink?' she says.

I shake my head. I stare at the food on my plate and my stomach churns.

'Gary,' she says. 'Are you all right, my man?'

I look up at her. 'I'm not hungry, Mum,' I say, and I push the plate away.

Mum tuts. She walks over to the sink and washes up her mug. 'I've got to go back to work now, Gary. I shan't be back till six, but your father'll be back about five.'

I snort. Like fuck he'll be back. Lazy bugger'll be in the Swan.

Mum gives me a look, like she knows what I'm

thinking. 'Just you have a think about what happened today, cos when your father gets home, he's gornta want a very stern word with you, young man.' She kisses me on the top of my head, picks up her keys and handbag, and then heads for the front door. Patch follows her. 'And don't you even think about going out of this house - you're grounded.'

Mum heaves the door open and then she's gone. Patch starts whining for a minute, then comes back through to the kitchen.

I sit at the kitchen table and stare at the cheese puffs on my plate. All the while I can feel it again - the pressure building in my head like someone's blowing up a fucking balloon in there. It gets worse and worse, so bad that I can't fucking stand it. If I don't do something, I'm gonna fucking well explode. I stand up, send my chair flying behind me. And before I can even think about what I'm doing, I pick up the plate and throw it at the wall.

It smashes. The sandwich sticks to the wall, then slides down and lands on the broken plate. The cheese puffs just scatter all over the place. Patch stands up and starts barking, crouching down. Then he goes over and sniffs the plate, gobbles down the bread. All I can do is stand there and stare at the mess and wish I hadn't done it. I turn, walk out of the kitchen and pull the front door open.

Zoë

The playing field's deserted. As I walk in along the gravel drive, there's a grim-looking building up ahead. 'The Wallingham Social Club'. It's empty. Closed. Depressing as hell.

I turn towards the playing field. Over on the far side, a man's walking a little yappy dog. And over to the right there's a play area with a great big tree trunk, like a telegraph pole, laid down for balancing on. Just beyond that there's a set of swings, with a boy sitting on one. The boy on the swing isn't swinging. He's just sitting there, looking down at the ground.

I walk over to the swings. I walk past the boy and sit on the swing next to his. He doesn't look up. He's about my age, maybe a year older. Quite big. Not fat, just big. He isn't much to look at. He's got a really round head and short fuzzy ginger hair. His face is covered in freckles. I look at him, try to catch his eye, but he just stares at the ground. He's wearing black trousers and a white short-sleeved shirt. It must be school uniform. It's Thursday. He should be at school now. God knows why he isn't. Must be skiving, I guess.

No matter how hard I stare at him, the boy doesn't look up. So I give up and start to swing instead, concentrate on swinging as high as I can. We used to do that at the park near where I live. Where I used to live. Till they changed the swings to the baby kind that only let you swing up to a certain height. Everyone said they changed them cos of this kid called Leon, cos he swung so high that the swing ended up going right up over the frame. Someone had to call an ambulance, so they say. But I reckon it's just a load of crap. They changed the swings cos they changed the swings, that's all.

Every now and then I glance at the boy as I'm swinging. He doesn't look at me. I don't think he's moved a muscle since I got here. After a while, I get bored and put my feet out to stop myself. And I look at the boy. It's like a challenge – I have to get him to look at me.

And he does. Slowly he lifts his head and looks straight at me. 'What's your problem?' he says. 'What you looking at?'

Wow! He talks. And he has an attitude all right. But I like that. He looks down at the ground again. I rack my brains for something to say, something that won't sound stupid, something that won't sound like I have a problem. But I can't think of anything. So I say, 'Sorry, I was staring, wasn't I?'

He looks confused.

'What's your name?' I say.

He looks up again, suspiciously. He doesn't say anything for ages – just stares at me like he's trying to figure me out. 'Gary,' he says really quietly. 'Gary Wood.' He has an accent. Must be a Norfolk accent.

I smile at him. But he's looking at the ground again. 'My name's Zoë.'

'Good for you,' he says, without looking up.

And now I don't know what to say, so I just sway gently on the swing and watch the man and the yappy dog cross the field. The man keeps throwing a stick for the dog to fetch. The dog fetches it each time, but then runs round the man, teasing him with the stick, not giving it back straight away.

I look back at Gary. He isn't staring at the ground any more. He's gazing out into the distance, across the field.

'Do you go to school?'

He looks down at the ground. He makes a sound. A grunt.

'I'll take that as a yes, then,' I say.

He just looks at the ground.

'Which school?'

'Wendham,' he says without looking up.

'Really?' I say. 'I'm supposed to be starting there next week. What's it like?'

He shrugs. 'Pile of shit.' A smile creeps across the corner of his mouth. Then it goes again.

I laugh. 'All schools are shit, Gary!' I say. 'You'll have to be more specific than that. Is it like a big steaming pile of dung or just a little squirty dribble?'

Gary smiles. He looks up at me. He kind of snorts, laughing. 'It's a massive stinking bloody cowpat!'

I laugh too.

Gary looks away again.

'So why aren't you there, then? Are you skiving or something?'

He doesn't look up. His jaw sort of clenches.

I stop my swing from swaying and look at Gary. What *is* wrong with him? He looks so angry, like there's something awful going on in his head. 'Have you been chucked out or something?'

His jaw clenches even more. He concentrates on looking at the ground so much that it looks like his eyes are gonna pop out of their sockets.

'It's OK,' I say. 'You can tell me. I'm no angel, either. I've been thrown out of schools before.' Which is a lie.

He looks up at me slowly. 'Have you?'

I nod. The secret to a good lie is to give a couple of details, make it seem real. 'Yeah. Once,' I say. 'Just for the day, though.'

Gary keeps looking at me. I think he doesn't know whether to believe me or not. 'Honestly?'

I nod again. 'Yeah. I got caught smoking by a teacher. What about you?'

He looks out across the field, at where the man with the yappy dog was before. 'I hit someone.'

I don't really know what to say. So I just nod my head. 'I've never done that,' I say. Which is the truth.

Gary doesn't reply. He stares out across the field. The wind gusts across it. I shiver.

'Who'd you hit?'

His face tenses up again. He turns and looks at me. 'What's with all these questions?' He says it quietly, but through gritted teeth. He stares at me for a couple of seconds.

'I'm just asking,' I say. 'You don't have to answer. I thought you might want to talk about it, that's all. I would if it was me.'

He takes a deep breath, closes his eyes for a second. 'This kid called Paul Knaggs.'

I smile at him. 'Did he deserve it?'

Gary shrugs his shoulders. 'Don't know,' he says. Then he looks angry again. 'Yeah, he did.'

'So they chucked you out?'

He nods. 'Yeah, till next week.'

'That's when I'm starting,' I say.

He sort of half nods his head. But I wouldn't say he looks interested.

'So how come you're sitting in the park? If I got sent home from school I'd get grounded for, like, my whole life.'

He shrugs again. 'No one knows I'm here. Mum had to go back to work, so I just come down here.'

'What about your dad?'

He doesn't answer. He shrugs his shoulders.

'So you just gonna sit here and look at the ground all afternoon?'

'Probably.'

We're silent. So's the field, except for a crow cawing somewhere.

'Is this where everyone hangs out, then?' I say after a while.

He shrugs. And then he shivers. He has goosebumps on his arms. He gets up from the swing. He starts to walk off, across the field.

'Where are you going?' I call after him.

He doesn't turn round. 'Home,' he says. 'I'm hungry.'

Gary

I'd leave school now, if they'd let me. I can't see no point in it. How's learning French or science or whatever gonna help me? I should be doing a job, earning some money. I couldn't care less what job it was, as long as it was as far away from Wendham High School as possible.

When I was little, I only had one thing in my head. I wanted to be a farmer. I remember when I was about three or four and Dad took me to work with him. We used to drive round the fields in a tractor, me sitting on Dad's lap. He used to let me steer it. That was the best feeling in the world. I felt like a grown-up. I was the one driving the tractor. In my head, it was my farm, I was the farmer.

I had a whole farm at home as well. A toy farm, I mean. Fields, fences, animals, sheds, barns – the whole lot. But it was always the tractors that I used to play with most. I've still got them all somewhere. In the loft, I think.

Dad used to work for Henry Walpole on a farm in Wallingham. He was Henry's dairyman. Basically he just looked after the cattle for Henry. He'd be up really early, get the cows ready for milking. When I was old enough, he took me to work with him most days in the holidays. I used to love it. I'd have quit school then if I'd been allowed to, and just worked on the farm.

And when I got home, I'd play with my toy farm – run it like a proper farm, just like Henry's farm. Henry's farm *was* a proper farm back then, before it went downhill, before it became an overgrown scrap-yard. I'd even pretend to go to market and buy new animals, sell the milk, slaughter the male calves. Everything. Sounds stupid, doesn't it? But that's all I knew. I thought I was gonna end up working on a farm when I grew up. Didn't even think of anything else. But then everything changed, didn't it?

I don't know what I'll do when I leave school now. Work in a factory like Mum, I s'pose. Probably end up slaughtering chickens or something, like all the other losers round here.

FRIDAY

Zoë

My stuff is now unpacked, just like Mum and Dad wanted. The boxes have officially been emptied, moved out of my room and stacked on the landing. True, most of my clothes are now in a big heap in the middle of my floor. And my walls are still blank and blue and yuck and covered in blobs of Blu-tack. But at least I've done what I was asked. It'll stop them nagging me. For a bit.

I go downstairs and Mum and Dad are unpacking in the kitchen. No surprise there. Dad's so engrossed in unwrapping cutlery that he doesn't even look at me. But Mum stops what she's doing, brushes her hair away from her face with the back of her hand and smiles.

'I'm going out for a little while,' I say.

'OK. Is your stuff unpacked, Zoë?'

I nod.

'Oh well, OK then, I s'pose. Just for a bit, though, love. Make sure you're back by half twelve for lunch. We need to go and get your uniform and do some shopping this afternoon.'

I sigh and fold my arms.

'Don't be like that, Zo,' Mum says.

I roll my eyes.

Mum smiles at me. A sort of sad smile.

'Can I borrow some money, Mum?'

'What for?' she says.

'To go to the shop. There's nothing else to do in Wallingham.'

Mum sighs. But she goes over to the worktop and grabs her purse anyway. She hands me £1.

'Is that all?'

Mum gives me a look. She shakes her head, like she can't believe I said that.

'OK. Ta,' I say, and I turn and head for the front door.

'Where are you going to be?' Mum calls after me.

'I dunno. Playing field, probably,' I say as I open the door.

'Have you got your mobile phone?' she asks.

I step outside and shut the door behind me.

* * *

He's there again, in the playing field. The boy on the swing. Gary. He's on the swing, gazing at nothing. I thought he would be. He doesn't look up when I walk towards him. He just sits there, like he has all the worries of the world bouncing around his head.

Gary isn't wearing his school uniform today. He's wearing camouflage combats and an army jacket instead. Back in Morden, there was a kid at my primary school who used to wear army gear all the time. Michael Brooks was his name. He was weird; he used to sit in lessons and make stupid squeaking and screeching and crashing noises. And he liked guns *way* more than is healthy. Some people said he had a replica gun that he used to shoot cats up the arse with. He wanted to be a soldier when he grew up. If that isn't weird then I don't know what is.

'All right, Gary. You off to a war or something?' I say as I sit on the free swing.

He looks up. 'What?'

I point at his clothes. 'Camouflage. You look like you're in the army or something,' I say with a smile.

He looks down at his clothes. 'Very funny.' He blushes.

'Sorry, crap joke,' I say. 'Anyway, camo is very "in" in Norfolk this season, so I hear!'

He doesn't laugh. He just does that staring thing

again. It's a bit annoying.

'So how come you're here again today, Gary? Did your mum just let you out?'

He shakes his head. 'She don't know I'm here,' he says. 'She's at work.'

I start swinging gently and look out across the playing field. It's pretty much empty again, except for a woman with a dog. It looks like the yappy dog I saw yesterday. Maybe it is. The woman doesn't throw a stick for the dog, though. She has it on a lead. The yappy dog looks like it's sulking. It probably likes fetching sticks better than being on a lead. I would if I were a dog.

I stop swinging and look at Gary. He's doing exactly what he seems to do best: sitting staring into space. 'You said you go to Wendham High School, didn't you?' I say.

He looks a little uncomfortable. He makes a grunting noise that I think means 'yes'.

'What year are you in, Gary?'

He looks at me. 'Year Ten. Why?'

I smile. I knew it. 'Honestly? You're in year ten?'

He nods his head and makes this face at the same time, like, *'Yeah, what's it to you?'*

'That's so cool! I'm in year ten too. We might be in the same tutor group.'

He looks away and doesn't say anything.

'What are the teachers like?' I ask him.

He sighs.

'Hey, are there any fit boys in year ten?'

Gary turns and looks at me. 'How the fuck would I know?'

'Well, you've got eyes, haven't you?' I say.

'I'm not fucking queer,' he says. And he looks away. Again.

For God's sake, what's his problem? 'Don't be so homophobic! You don't have to be gay to see whether someone's fit or not!'

He doesn't look round.

'Like, for instance, I could tell you which girls are fit. That doesn't make me a lesbian, does it?'

He slowly looks round. He's smirking. I can't help but smile back.

'What's so funny?' I say.

He stops smirking. 'Nothing,' he says. And then in a quieter voice he says, 'You might be a lezza, for all I know.' His cheeks go red.

I laugh and smile at him. We sit in silence for a while. I think it's clear that I'm not going to get any inside info from Gary on who's fit and who's not. Oh well. I'll find out soon enough.

It doesn't take long for the silence to do my head in, though. 'So are the teachers strict, then?'

Gary sits and stares.

'Back at my old school, we had this English teacher called Mr McCartney. He used to make us stand up when we were answering a question. Can you believe that?'

No reaction.

'He was so creepy. He'd call all the boys "young man" and all the girls "young lady". So patronising.'

Gary sighs and folds his arms.

I make a point of looking at him and then carrying on. If he has a problem, he can tell me. 'Mr McCartney was so old-fashioned, right, when you did something wrong, he'd make you stay in at break-time and he'd give you this long lecture about how "young people have no respect for anyone, least of all themselves" and blah-blah-blah. And then he'd make you copy out the dictionary. And if he thought it wasn't your neatest handwriting he'd . . .'

I stop because Gary's turning his head slowly towards me. He looks at me with bulging, angry eyes. He looks like the Incredible Hulk as he's about to turn green. 'Will you shut the fuck up?' he says. 'I don't want to talk about school. I don't want to hear about your bloody old teachers. I hate school. Just leave me alone!'

He turns away and stares at that same patch of ground again. He's gonna burn a hole in the ground if he keeps staring at it like that. He looks like he might cry. But he doesn't. I feel guilty. I was trying to provoke him. I shouldn't have done that.

'I'm sorry. I didn't mean anything. I was just trying to be friendly. If you want me to go away, just say.'

He doesn't say anything. He just sits there. He looks so unbelievably angry. It's difficult to look at him. It makes me feel uncomfortable.

I sigh. 'Oh, me and my big mouth again.' Maybe I should just say nothing, get up and leave him to feel sorry for himself. It's obvious I'm not making him feel any better.

But I don't leave. I want to know what the matter is. I want to help him. I sit, look away from Gary and try to think of something that'll take his mind off whatever's bothering him so much. All I can come up with is, 'So, are you gonna take me on a tour of Wallingham today or what?'

He doesn't look at me. He just shakes his head.

'Please?' I say. 'Why not?'

Gary doesn't move. Doesn't even shake his head. But his stomach rumbles. He blushes.

I remember the chocolate bars in my pocket. I bought them in the shop earlier. I have an idea. 'Hey, I'll tell you what. You show me the sights of Wallingham and I'll give you some chocolate!'

He looks at me, suspicious. But I can tell he's interested.

I pull one of the Snickers bars from my pocket and dangle it in front of his face. 'Deal?' I say. 'Or no deal?'

He looks at the chocolate and then at me, like he's not sure whether to trust me. Eventually he sort of smiles. 'All right.' He grabs the chocolate bar. 'Deal!'

We slip off the swings and begin walking across the empty playing field. The grass is wet and my trainers soak up the water like sponges. There isn't much there apart from a couple of rusty-looking football goalposts and a little taped-off cricket square. It doesn't take long for Gary to eat his Snickers – maybe three bites. Then he looks at mine, which I haven't opened yet.

'Here, go on, have it,' I say. 'You look hungry.'

He looks at me for a second and then grabs the bar off me. He tears the wrapper and takes a massive bite.

'Doesn't your mum feed you?' I say.

Gary doesn't say anything. He just looks at me. He stops chewing and looks embarrassed.

I smile at him. 'It was a joke,' I say. 'Eat!'

Then he goes back to eating the bar, just much more slowly than before.

We walk on in silence. I've sort of run out of things to say again. It isn't easy talking to someone who doesn't really talk back.

We've nearly come to the end of the playing field. There's a hedge in front of us, and behind that I can just see the tops of some houses. They look like our new house: square and boring. Lego homes.

Gary leads the way over to the right, where there's a narrow mud path that leads off the field into a little wood. The path isn't very wide, so I follow behind him.

'Where are we going?'

'Other side of the village,' he says.

'What, you mean this place has more than one side?'

It was meant to be a joke, but Gary doesn't laugh. He turns round and looks at me, like he doesn't quite understand. He nods. 'Yeah.'

'So what's on the other side of the village, then?'

He shrugs. 'Just some fields and stuff. Not much. The church.'

'Wow,' I say under my breath. 'Exciting.'

And then we walk in silence for a while. There are loads of muddy puddles on the path that I have to jump over or walk round. Gary just walks straight through them. He has big black boots on – army boots or something. He looks like Action Man in all that camo gear. I wonder if he's got a cord coming out of his back to make him talk, too. If he has, maybe I should give it a tug.

After a while the woods thin out and there are the back gates of a few houses on either side of the path. The path's wider now, made out of stones instead of mud. I quicken my pace to keep up with Gary.

'You walk fast, don't you?'

Gary nods his head.

And there's silence again. Gary gets to the end of the path first and stops by the edge of the road. He looks to the right and stares. He looks nervous, sort of.

'What's the matter?'

He doesn't answer. He just points down the road at the vehicle that's heading towards us. A mobility scooter, driving right down the middle of the road. Gary stands there and waits for it to get closer. He looks uncomfortable. Slowly, the scooter draws nearer. And then it stops, right in front of us. An old man sits on the scooter, wearing a trilby hat and a pair of the most enormous shades. They cover most of his face. He smiles at Gary.

'All right, Gary, boy,' he says in a Norfolk accent.

'All right.'

'You not at school today, my man?'

Gary blushes. 'No.'

'Why on earth not, boy?'

Gary looks down at his black boots. 'Been excluded for fighting,' he mumbles.

The old man chuckles. And then the chuckle becomes a cough that lasts for ages. The man has to pat his chest a couple of times, to stop himself from coughing. He spits something into a hankie. 'Oh dear, 'scuse me. Take a tip, children: never smoke! Well, Gary, boy, I hope you gave the other feller a good hiding anyhow!'

Gary keeps looking at his shoes and nods.

The man on the scooter chuckles again. 'That's the spirit. Just like your father. He was always scrapping an' all.'

Gary looks up at him for a second.

'So how come you're roaming the streets, then, my man? I should have thought you're in enough trouble already if you've been sent home from school. Aren't your mother and father cross with you?'

Gary shifts uncomfortably.

'Is your mother at home today, boy?'

Gary shakes his head.

'Father?'

Gary shakes his head again.

The old man shakes his too. 'Well, I don't know if you should be out here, boy. I hope your father don't catch you. Otherwise it'll be you who's getting a good hiding!'

The man on the scooter laughs again. Then he looks away from Gary, straight at me, like he's noticing me for the first time. He lifts his enormous sunglasses up and then looks at me, starting at the top of my head and slowly going down my whole body. Then his eyes travel back up again. He licks his lips. It makes me feel sick. I shiver.

'Who's this lovely young lady, Gary?' he says. 'I never seen her before.'

Gary's blushing. He doesn't say anything.

'Come on, boy. Cat got your tongue?'

Gary shakes his head. He looks at me. 'I can't remember your name,' he says. 'Sorry.'

I feel a jolt in my chest somewhere. I give Gary a look. And then I turn away from him and look at the dirty old man. 'Zoë,' I say. 'I'm Zoë.'

The dirty old man smiles a rotten-toothed grin. 'Well, Zoë,' he says, 'I must go and post a letter. Make sure young Gary here stays out of trouble, won't you?'

And then he turns his head, and his mobility scooter buzzes off down the road.

Me and Gary walk on in silence, out into the countryside. A few fields, some hedges and a couple of tiny roads for as far as the eye can see. And the sky. The big grey sky. All the while, I want to say something like '*I can't believe you couldn't even remember my name.*' But I don't. I just trot along behind him and try to keep up.

'Where're we going?'

'Dunno,' Gary says. 'Farm maybe.'

In my head I yawn at the prospect. But I follow Gary anyway, along the narrow road, past the fields. We walk right down the middle of the road. It feels as if we're being rebellious. Doing this in Morden would be suicidal. But in Wallingham the roads always seem to be empty. No cars. Ever.

We don't say anything. Gary just marches us along. He walks as though he's in the army. Big strides. But his head and shoulders are always stooped, like he's got something bad going on in his head. I guess maybe he has.

'Are you all right, Gary?'

He kind of half looks round, but not at me. And then he mumbles something. I think it's 'yeah'.

Another silence. We keep marching down the middle of the road. I look at the fields. The one on the right is filled with something yellow, something that stinks. The one on the left is covered in long grass and old tractors and machines that I don't know the names of. They're all rusting and falling apart, like a tractor graveyard.

'Why's that field full of rusty tractors?' I ask.

Gary slows a little, looks over the hedge into the field. He looks like he knows what he's looking at. 'That's Henry's field,' he says.

'Oh.'

'He was a lazy bugger,' Gary says. 'Never fixed his bloody machinery. He's dead now, though, anyhow.'

We walk a little further up the road, to a chained gate on the left-hand side. Gary looks both ways and then climbs the gate.

I look at him. 'Are we allowed to do this?'

He shrugs. He has a very faint smile on his face. 'My dad used to work here,' he says. 'No one uses it any more. No one's gonna see us.'

I look along the road. There's no one coming in either direction. I step forward and climb the gate.

Gary smiles at me.

'So your dad's a farmer?'

The smile fades from Gary's face. He starts walking across the field.

I follow him.

'He was a dairyman,' Gary says. 'Worked for Henry.'

'Oh,' I say. 'So what does he do now?'

He shrugs. 'Handyman,' he says. 'Odd jobs.'

The grass is really long and wet in the field. Doesn't really make a difference to my trainers cos they're already soaked, but now the bottoms of my jeans are getting wet as well. Right across the field I can see a bunch of buildings and a little concrete farmyard. I'm no expert, but I'd guess that one's the farmhouse and the other's a barn. Don't know about the others, though. Even from this distance, I can tell they've all seen better days. They look like they're crumbling away, like eroded cliffs or something.

We march straight across the field, towards the buildings. We stop in the big barn. It's full of farm machinery, some old and rusty like the stuff in the field, but some newer stuff that just looks dirty. Weeds are growing everywhere, and old sacks and boxes and stuff lie all around. It stinks in here. It's difficult to know where the smell's coming from. I think it might be the straw. Or maybe it's rats. Whatever it is, it doesn't smell good.

Gary climbs up on to a tractor and sits in the cab or cockpit or whatever you call it, dangling his legs over the side. I look around for a box that doesn't look too dirty and then I sit.

'Does anyone live here?'

Gary shakes his head. 'Nah,' he says. 'There's a row going on in Henry's family about who should have it. Stupid dickhead didn't leave no will. Don't belong to no one yet. I don't s'pose they'd want to move in, though, after what happened . . .'

I nod as though I have a clue what he's talking about. But I don't, so I change the subject. 'Who was that man on the scooter?'

'Herbert,' Gary says.

'He gave me the creeps.'

'He's all right.'

'Did you see the way he looked me up and down?'

Gary doesn't say anything.

'Is he a pervert or something?'

Gary shakes his head. 'Herbert's just an old man,' he says. 'He's all right.'

And then we sit in silence for what seems like eternity. I pick up stones from the floor and start to throw them at a bucket. They keep missing the bucket, bouncing off the ground and hitting the tractor with a *ping*.

'Not much of a shot, are you?'

I look up at Gary. 'Can you do any better?'

He jumps down from the tractor, crouches down next to me and grabs a handful of stones. And then he throws them, one after the other. *CLUNK. CLUNK. CLUNK. CLUNK. CLUNK. CLUNK.*

They all go in.

'Very impressive.'

Gary smiles modestly for a second. 'Not bad.'

I try throwing another. *CLUNK.* It hits the rim of the bucket and then bounces off.

And then it's quiet again. We seem to have a lot of these silences. They're sort of awkward. And Gary never seems to fill them. So I leave this one and just stare around the barn, trying to work out how long it must have been since Henry died. Everything's started to rust, so it must be quite a while. And there are lots of weeds growing up through everything. I'd say no one's sorted this place out in at least two years. At least.

Eventually I get an urge to say something – anything.

'You don't say much, do you?' I say. I regret it as

soon as it comes out of my mouth.

Gary goes red. He doesn't look at me.

'Sorry,' I say. 'What I mean is, don't you want to know who I am? Don't you want to know where I come from?'

'S'pose,' he says. But then he sits there silently, staring into space and doesn't ask me a thing.

I sigh. And I wait for a while, for Gary to ask me about myself. But he doesn't, so I get up, dust down my jeans and walk over to the entrance of the barn. I look at the farmhouse. 'Have you ever been in there?' I ask.

'What?'

'The farmhouse. Have you ever been in there?'

Gary jumps down from the tractor and walks over towards me. 'Of course. Loads of times. Dad used to work for Henry.'

I look at the house. Apart from the fact that a breeze might topple it over, it looks quite nice. It's big and built from bricks. I bet it was cosy, once upon a time. I can imagine a farmer's wife in there, baking bread and doing all that farmer's wife stuff. It's the kind of house I imagined when Mum and Dad said we were gonna move to the country.

'Can we go in there?' I ask.

Gary looks at the house and shakes his head.

'Oh, come on,' I say. 'Why not?'

'It's not right,' he says. 'It ain't ours.'

'Neither's this barn, but we're in here, aren't we?'

Gary screws up his face as though he's thinking hard about something and then he shakes his head. 'It's Henry's house,' he says. 'It's personal. We shouldn't. That's for Henry's family, not us.' He goes back and sits on the tractor.

For whatever reason, I suddenly think of Mum and Dad. I'm supposed to be home by half twelve. 'Have you got a watch, Gary?' I ask.

Gary nods and then looks at his watch. 'Quarter to one,' he says.

'Oh no!' I say. 'See you later.'

David

It's windy. And we're lined up by the pavilion on the field for PE. Our school field must be the windiest place on the face of the planet. Honestly. So I'm jogging up and down on the spot, pulling the sleeves of my football shirt over my fingers, trying to stay warm. Mr Lawson, our PE teacher, stands in front of us. Sometimes we call him 'Bumble' on account of the fact that he has this old tracksuit – it's from the seventies or eighties – that's black with big orange stripes, like a bumblebee. He's rubbing his hands together and looking along the line at us.

'OK, boys,' he says. 'Game of football today. Alfie, you can be a captain. Over here, please. And, Dougie, you too. Over here on the other side of me.'

Dougie and Alfie go and stand by Mr Lawson, one on each side. It's always them who're captains, cos they're both on the school team. Dougie's *way* better than Alfie, though. He plays up front and scores shed-loads of goals. I'm on the team as well, but I usually end up being a sub, so Mr Lawson never picks me as captain in PE.

Dougie and Alfie take it in turns to choose players for their teams, picking the best footballers and the hardest kids first, leaving all the pebbleheads and the fat kids till last. I end up on Alfie's side. Knaggs is on Dougie's side.

'Right, lads, go and get warmed up on the pitch,' Bumble says.

'But, Mr Lawson,' says Dougie, 'they've got eleven players and we've only got ten, sir.'

Bumble looks at both teams, from one player to the next. You can see him mouthing numbers as he counts up the players. 'Never mind,' he says. 'It looks fair enough to me.' And he walks away towards the pavilion like he's solved the problem.

Alfie grabs a ball and leads our team to the pitch, right over to the half that's furthest away. It's the best half to have, cos it means you get to kick downhill. Dougie's team'll be even more pissed off when they get to the pitch, cos not only have they got fewer players, but they've also got the worst half. But they're not moving at the moment. They're still standing outside the pavilion, waiting for Bumble to come back out.

'Come on, lads, let's warm up,' Alfie says. And he kicks the ball to me.

I take it straight out to the wing and put in a cross. I hit it sweetly and the ball floats into the box and Alfie goes up for the header.

BOOF!

The ball ends up in the back of the net.

After a few minutes, Bumble comes out of the pavilion holding the ball and dribbles it into the middle of the pitch. Dougie and his team follow him out. They're all having a moan at him. Dougie and Knaggs look fed up. And Bumble's just ignoring them. He stands right on the centre spot and blows his whistle.

'Everyone come into the centre circle!' he shouts.

So we all walk in.

'OK,' he says, as the last few people make it into the middle. 'We'll swap ends to even it up a little.'

'Ah, sir!' we all say together.

'No arguments,' Bumble says. 'Swap ends and let's get this game started.'

'But we haven't got a keeper on our side,' Dougie says. 'Look, they've got Ed *and* Callum on their side.

Can't we swap someone for them?'

Bumble shakes his head. 'You picked your side, Dougie. Don't blame me.'

'But no one wants to go in goal, sir,' Knaggs says. 'We need a goalie.'

Bumble shakes his head again.

'But how are we gonna play without a goalie?'

'I don't know and I don't care,' says Bumble. 'Pretend you've got a goalie. Just swap ends and let's get started now.'

Alfie leads our team over to the other side of the pitch and we get into position. Knaggs and Dougie and the rest of their team drag themselves out of the centre circle and into their half. They get themselves ready. But they don't look happy. And no one's gone in goal. This should be easy.

Bumble picks the ball up and places it on the centre spot. He puts his foot on the ball, like he's the captain of England or something. 'Dougie, your team can kick off,' he says. And he steps away from the ball.

Dougie and Mike step forward. I jog on the spot to keep warm.

Mr Lawson blows the whistle.

Mike touches the ball to Dougie. He plays it behind him to Knaggs. Knaggs takes the ball and turns, towards his own goal. He starts dribbling with the ball, in and out of his own teammates. Some of them try to tackle him, some of them just look at him and some laugh. And then, with a thundering shot, Knaggs lets the ball fly at his own goal. The net ripples.

'YYYYYYEEEEEESSSSS!' Knaggs cries. He raises his arms to the sky, like he's thanking God. He falls to his knees and kisses the ground.

Both teams start laughing.

Bumble starts blowing his whistle. He runs down the pitch towards Knaggs. 'What on earth was that?' he shouts. He stands above Knaggs, who is still on his knees.

'What?' says Knaggs.

'What the bloody hell are you playing at, boy?'

Knaggs stands up. He looks at Bumble like he's confused, like, *'What's all the fuss?'*

'Explain yourself!' Bumble says. He looks angry.

Knaggs shrugs. 'You said to pretend we had a keeper, sir,' Knaggs says, all innocent. 'So I did. I passed back to the imaginary goalkeeper, sir. But he's crap and he didn't save it!'

We all fall about laughing. I sink to my knees, I'm laughing so much.

Bumble blows his whistle. 'Stop laughing this instant!'

So we do. Sort of. We just snigger instead.

'Right, Mr Knaggs,' Bumble says. 'I'm sending you off for that. Go and sit by the side.'

'But, sir,' Knaggs says, 'I was only doing what you said!' He shrugs his shoulders and acts like he can't understand why he's been sent off. But he does what he's told. He walks over to the side of the pitch and sits down. And as soon as Bumble's back is turned, he sticks his fingers up at him and gets another laugh.

It's not much of a game after that. Bumble doesn't seem interested, doesn't blow his whistle or anything. And no one on the pitch can take it seriously. And besides, eleven against nine isn't fair. When Alfie puts our team 3–1 up, Joe walks off the pitch as well, goes and sits with Knaggs. Bumble doesn't say a word. And after a bit, I do the same.

'That was hilarious,' I say. 'Bumble looked mad!'

Knaggs smiles at me. 'Rule number one,' he says. 'Never mess with the Knaggster!'

Zoë

Shopping was a complete nightmare. The uniform for Wendham High School sucks badly. They have black blazers with shabby little badges on them, black-and-grey-and-blue-striped ties, black jumpers, black skirts, black tights and flat black shoes. Or at least that's what it said on the list that Mum had. If I wore that much black at home, she'd have a fit. She'd tell me to brighten myself up. But, anyway, I bet no one in year ten actually dresses like that – teachers never notice if you've got heels on your shoes, or if you wear trainers, or your tie's too short. Back at Morden we had a vote on our uniform. We chose to have sweatshirts and to allow black trainers, as long as they didn't have a big logo on them. It wasn't exactly fashionable, but at least it wasn't as bad as Wendham. And at least we had a say in it.

After getting the uniform we went to the supermarket. Mum and Dad went in while I sat in the car. They were in there for hours. I listened to my MP3 player and sat there, watching all the Norfolk people walking around. Most of them looked inbred. Rianna was right.

Mum and Dad eventually came back out with a load of economy stuff.

Mum said, 'We'll just have to put up with it for a while, until we get ourselves sorted.'

But if she seriously expects me to go to school with a lunch box full of economy bread and economy cereal bars and economy yogurt, she's wrong. I'll throw it in a hedge and go to the canteen instead.

David

'Tea's ready, Ollie, David,' Mum shouts up the stairs.

I switch off my telly, clomp down the stairs and into the kitchen. Lasagne and oven chips. Mum's speciality! I sit down at the table.

Dad's already there, putting some brown sauce on his chips. 'Have a good day today, Davey?'

I shrug. 'All right, I s'pose. Not bad.' I pick up the tomato sauce and squeeze some on to my plate.

'What did you have today?' Dad says. 'Science? Maths? PE? Geography?'

I've just put a chip in my mouth, so I nod my head in the right place instead.

'PE?' Dad says.

I nod again as I swallow my chip. 'Football.'

Dad smiles at me. 'Did you win?'

I nod. I think about the game earlier. I don't want Dad to know anything about the game other than that we won. He'd go mental if he knew what we'd done.

Fortunately Ollie comes into the kitchen, so I don't have to explain today's PE lesson to Dad. Ollie sits down at the table without looking at anyone, without saying anything. He just does that thing where he lets his fringe cover his face.

'All right, Olls,' Dad says. 'How was your day?'

Ollie picks up his knife and fork. He shrugs. 'All right.' He leans his head and lets his hair fall even further across his face.

Mum brings cups of tea over to the table. She gives one to me and Dad first, then she goes back to the side and gets one for her and Ollie. She sits down and picks up her knife and fork.

'City are at home tomorrow, boys,' Dad says. 'Paul at work's going away for the weekend, so we can borrow his season tickets if you want.'

I nod my head eagerly. 'Cool. Leicester, isn't it?'

'Yeah,' Dad says. 'Should be three points, I reckon. Ollie, you fancy coming?'

Ollie shakes his head and showers us all in dandruff. 'Working,' he says. He doesn't like football anyway. He just likes depressing music and comics.

'Oh, all right. Just me and you then, Davey-boy,' Dad says. 'Hey, I reckon we should take our boots – we might even get a game!'

I sort of laugh, just to be polite. It must be about the thousandth time I've heard Dad make that joke. It wasn't even funny the first time he said it.

It's quiet for a while. Everyone's munching their food and slurping their tea.

'Oh, David,' Mum says all of a sudden, like she's just remembered something important. 'I was talking to Margaret at work today . . .'

I stop chewing. I look down at my plate. I can feel my cheeks going red. I feel guilty already. I know what she's gonna say.

'She got called away from work yesterday, to the school,' Mum says, all casual. 'Didn't see her again till today. She says Gary's been excluded.'

Shit! I want the earth to swallow me up. My stomach ties itself in a knot. I have to think of something to say. 'Yeah' is all I can come up with.

'She's very worried about him, David, you know.'

I cut a bit of lasagne that I know I'm not gonna be able to eat now.

'He had a fight, so Margaret said,' Mum says. She puts her knife and fork down on her plate and looks at me.

I pretend to be interested in my food, push some

chips round my plate. The kitchen is quiet. I feel uncomfortable.

'Did you see what happened?' Mum goes on.

I shrug. 'Yeah. He hit someone after science yesterday.' I look up at Mum. My heart's racing.

Mum picks up her cup of tea and cradles it in her hands. 'I probably shouldn't be saying this but the school want him to go and have some counselling,' she says. She sounds really concerned.

I nod my head and look at my plate, like this really has nothing to do with me.

Mum picks up her knife and fork. But she doesn't eat. She just looks at me. I play with my food again.

'Margaret thinks someone might be bullying Gary,' Mum says.

The knot in my stomach tightens. Next to me, Ollie sighs and shakes his head. He bangs his knife and fork around on his plate.

Mum looks at him for a second, but then she turns back to me. 'Have you seen anyone bullying Gary?' she says.

I shake my head. 'No,' I lie.

Mum puts her knife and fork back down on the table. 'Well, Margaret's convinced he's being bullied. Will you keep an eye out for me, David? He's back on Monday. She's ever so worried about him . . .'

I nod my head and push my plate into the middle of the table.

SATURDAY

Zoë

Saturday morning. Dad's taken the removal van back to Joe in London. I wanted to go too, wanted to go and see Jodie and my mates. But hey, guess what? As if any guesswork is needed. They said no. I have to stay here, in the middle of nowhere, where I know no one, where I have nothing to do.

Mum's in the lounge watching a cookery programme, making new curtains out of some grim flowery material. I need to get out of this house. So I go downstairs.

'I'm going out, Mum.'

She looks up from the sewing machine. She looks tired. 'Oh, OK, dear,' she says. 'Have you put your clothes away yet?'

'Yeah,' I lie.

'And you've hung up your uniform?'

I nod.

'OK, then,' she says. 'Where are you off to?'

'Dunno,' I say. 'Playing field maybe.'

'That's a good idea, love,' she says. 'You might even meet some kids who go to your new school.'

'Hmm, maybe,' I mumble. And then I remember Gary and a wicked thought goes through my head. 'Actually, I've already met someone.'

'Have you?' Mum says. She sounds surprised. 'When was that?'

'Yesterday,' I say. 'And the day before.'

'Oh,' says Mum. She says it casual. But I can see it on her face – the cogs turning round, the alarm bells starting to ring. 'Shouldn't she have been at school?'

'It was a he,' I say. 'And he wasn't at school because he got sent home for hitting someone.'

I watch the look on Mum's face. It's a picture. I can tell she thinks I'm already falling in with the wrong crowd, like the Jodie situation all over again. Only this time it's worse, cos there's a boy. She looks horrified.

'Oh,' she says, trying to stay calm. 'I'm not sure I like the sound of him. What's his name?'

'Gary,' I say. 'Anyway, Mum, I'm going out. See you later.'

'Make sure you take your phone, Zoë. I had no idea where you were yesterday. You know I worry.'

'I've got it,' I say. And I get out of the front door as quickly as I can, before she changes her mind about letting me out.

The playing field is nowhere near as empty as it was on Thursday and Friday. There's a door open at the social club and someone's setting out tables and chairs inside. On the field, a couple of little kids are playing football. There's no sign of the yappy dog, though. Or Gary.

But Gary's swing *has* got a boy on it. A different boy. A boy in a cap. He isn't sitting staring into space. He's standing up on the swing, swinging it as high and as fast as it'll go. He's shouting as well. There's another boy on the swing next to him, much taller. He's standing up too. They look like they're having a race or something. The boy on Gary's swing jumps off as he swings forward. He lands a few feet in front and tumbles over. And the tall boy on the other swing follows. They stand up and laugh. They look like skaters, from what they're wearing. Probably about my age, I guess. The one in the cap's not bad-looking, either. A bit short, but not bad. Maybe there is a good side to Norfolk after all. I walk over to them.

'Excuse me,' I say.

'Well, *hello*,' says the boy in the cap. The boys look at each other and laugh. The boy in the cap winces and touches the side of his face. He has a bruise around his cheekbone.

'This is gonna sound really random,' I say. 'But do you know someone called Gary?'

They look at each other. 'Depends. Gary who?' says the one with the cap.

'I can't remember his last name,' I say. 'He's quite tall, fuzzy hair. I think he said he goes to Wendham High School. Year ten?'

The boys look at each other. They laugh. I'm not sure if they're laughing at me or not, but I don't like it.

'Does he have ginger hair and a head like a giant cheesy Wotsit? Talks like a farmer?' says the boy in the cap.

The tall boy bursts out laughing, almost spits all over the place.

I laugh as well. I guess he does look like a cheesy Wotsit. But I feel guilty for thinking it. 'I guess so. A little bit, yeah.'

They laugh. The boy in the cap winces again. 'You mean Gary Wood,' he says. 'The cheese-puff boy.'

'Yeah, I think so.'

'What do you wanna know about him for?'

I shrug my shoulders. 'I'm looking for him, that's all.'

The boys laugh again. I don't like the way they keep laughing at me. I know boys like this, back in London. Constantly taking the piss. And I've never liked them. Can't trust them. 'Look, do you know where he is or not?'

'Dead, I hope. Lying in a ditch,' says the cap boy.

I sigh, give them a dirty look and turn away. I head across the field, towards the path into the woods.

And then a voice calls from behind me, 'Hey, I wouldn't say no if you came looking for me!'

They both laugh again. *So* immature.

I turn and give them the middle finger.

He's there. At the farm. In the barn. Sitting in the tractor. Staring into space. The barn's even more of a mess than yesterday. It stinks like a toilet and there are fag butts and cider bottles lying around. I look at the bottles and then at Gary. They can't be his, surely. He's not old enough to get served. He doesn't look old enough. He's got bum fluff on his top lip. Unless maybe he robbed them from his house or something. I know plenty of kids that do . . .

'All right, Gary,' I say.

He nods his head. 'All right,' he says, without looking round.

I pick up the cider bottles and put them neatly at the side of the barn. I don't know why – just feels like the right thing to do. I sit down on an old box. 'I can't believe you're out again today,' I say.

Gary shrugs.

'I thought you'd be in a load of trouble. I would, if it was me. I'd be grounded.'

He looks at me and nods his head. He looks away again.

'Do your mum and dad work on Saturdays, then?' I ask.

Gary kind of snorts, like he's laughing. 'Something like that,' he says.

I smile at him. I think about what the boys in the playing field were saying about him just now. I want to ask him about them, about him. But I can't. Somehow, I get the feeling he wouldn't want to talk about it.

So I get up instead and I walk over to the entrance to the barn. I look at the farmhouse. I really want to go in there. I don't know why. I bet it's spooky. But I want to do it. Maybe I should come when Gary's not here, go in on my own.

Behind me I hear a thud and then footsteps. Gary appears at my shoulder. He looks at the house as well.

'Aren't you tempted to take a look?' I say.

Gary looks at the house for a second and then nods his head. 'A bit,' he says.

'Then why don't we?' I say. 'It won't hurt anyone.'

Gary shakes his head. 'No.'

'Well then, I'm gonna look in the window at least,' I say.

And I walk over to the house. Gary walks along behind me. I peer in through the dirty window. It's dark inside. Difficult to see much. But I can make out a really old-fashioned sink. There's an old electric cooker as well. Just beneath the window there's a table. It's got a filthy tablecloth on it. And there's a dirty glass and a knife and fork on it, like someone set the table and then never came back. And there's loads of dust everywhere. It looks a bit like the pictures they show on telly when they go to villages in Eastern Europe or somewhere.

'It's a bit skanky, isn't it?'

Gary peers through the window. 'That's Henry for you. He was a stingy bastard. That's what Dad always said.'

We step back from the house and just look around, at the farmyard with weeds growing up through it, at the barn, at the overgrown fields, at the dead tractors.

'What are you doing today, then?'

Gary shrugs. He looks at his watch. 'Gotta go home,' he says. 'Mum'll be back from work in a minute.'

'Where's your dad?'

Gary looks across the field. 'God knows,' he says.

He looks at his watch again. 'I gotta go,' he says. And he starts marching off.

'Hang on, I'll walk with you,' I say. And I jog a few steps to catch him up.

We walk in silence, pretty much. I ask Gary the odd question. And he gives me the odd one-word answer, or sometimes just a grunt. He doesn't ask me a single question. He still has no idea who I am, or where I come from. But then I've asked him, like, a bucketful of questions, and I still don't know anything about him, either. Maybe I should just stay quiet as well.

As we're walking down the middle of the road, back towards the village, I can see someone walking in the middle of the road, towards us. Gary kind of flinches when he sees him.

'What's the matter with you?' I say.

'Nothing,' Gary says. 'It's just him. That bloke. The medal man. I don't like him.'

I let out a little laugh. 'The medal man? What kind of a name's that?'

Gary shrugs.

'Why don't you like him?'

Gary shrugs again. 'He's weird. He stinks.'

As he gets closer, I can see why they call him the medal man. He has a medal hanging round his neck: a cheap piece of metal hanging on a dirty red, blue and white bit of cloth. There was a man like that in

Morden, except he only used to wear white clothes, nothing else. He even started painting himself white for a while – his face and hands and feet. But he disappeared after that. I heard he started drinking white gloss paint as well, to paint his insides. Everyone said he'd died.

The medal man hasn't noticed us. He looks like he's having a conversation with someone, arguing with them. But he's on his own. He's wearing this old light-blue suit that won't do up cos he's got a massive belly. And he's got an old grey sweatshirt. His beard's grey and greasy and stained yellow near his mouth. On his head he's wearing a cowboy hat. He looks totally mental.

Gary walks right on the edge of the road, to try and keep away from him. But I just keep walking down the middle of the road.

'Excuse me,' I say, as the medal man gets close.

He looks up. He's confused, a little scared. And Gary's right, he does stink. 'What?'

'I like your medal,' I say.

Gary stands behind the medal man. He wants to keep walking, I can tell. He's nervous.

The medal man holds up his medal and looks at it. He seems to be finding it hard to focus. He can't even stand without swaying.

'What did you get it for?'

He looks at me, tries to focus on my face. 'I was in the war,' he says. 'This . . .' He holds the medal out for me to see. It has two boys playing football engraved on it. 'This is for bravery!'

I laugh. But I feel guilty, so I stop.

The medal man carries on walking down the road. Every now and then he turns and looks at us.

'What did you do that for?' Gary says.

'What?'

'Talk to him!'

'Why shouldn't I?'

We start walking along again.

'He's mental,' Gary says. 'You shouldn't talk to him.'

I turn and look at Gary. He's saying all this like he's doing me a favour. 'Why shouldn't I? What harm's it gonna do?'

Gary doesn't answer. I know why. He's scared of the weird old man, that's why.

'Where does he live?'

'Who?' Gary says.

'The medal man, stupid.'

Gary shrugs. 'He's a tramp. He don't live nowhere.'

'A tramp?' I say. I had no idea tramps lived in the countryside. 'Where does he sleep, then? In the doorway of the shop?'

'Don't be stupid,' Gary says. 'Woods probably. Maybe a barn.'

We walk on in silence for a minute. We're coming in towards the village. I'm only about five minutes from home now. I think.

'Do you ever wonder why people like that end up being tramps?' I say.

Gary looks at me. He shakes his head. 'No.'

'I mean, he must've had a house. And then something happened and he couldn't deal with it, do you know what I mean? He must have run away from something. And now that's him. The medal man. Walking around the place on his own.'

Gary looks at me. He's thinking about it – you can see it on his face. 'S'pose.'

'It's sad, isn't it?'

Gary shrugs. 'I don't think it'd be so bad to run away,' he says quietly.

I look at him. He looks away. 'Yeah, maybe,' I say. 'I was gonna do it once, after my mum and dad found out I'd taken some money from the pot in the kitchen. I packed a load of stuff in a bag and snuck out of the flat. Only got as far as the end of the road, though. I felt too guilty.'

Gary looks at me. 'I think about it sometimes,' he says. 'Running away. I wouldn't be like the medal man. I wouldn't start drinking or anything like that. I'd just get away from this shithole, try and find a job or something.'

I smile at him. 'You wouldn't, though, would you?' I say.

He stops walking and looks at me. 'Probably not,' he says. And he turns and walks off to the left.

'Where are you going?'

'Home,' he says.

'Do you live down there?'

He stops walking, looks down at the ground. He nods.

'Can I come?'

He shakes his head.

'Why not?'

He doesn't answer. He just turns again and walks home.

David

'That was a dodgy ref, Davey,' Dad says, taking his eyes off the traffic jam to look at me.

I nod. I watch the wipers scrape drizzle off the windscreen.

'He cost us the game today,' Dad says. 'There's no way that was a penalty. That was ball to hand! Clearly. Do you reckon he left his white stick in the dressing room?'

I laugh. 'Yeah, I reckon,' I say. 'There's no way we're getting in the play-offs now, is there?'

Dad sighs. 'Looks that way, doesn't it?' And he puts the radio on.

We sit in traffic without talking, listening to the

full-time reports come in. I look out of the window, watch the Norwich fans dodge in and out of the traffic on their way back towards the town. And as I'm staring into space, the Ipswich report comes in. They won 3–1 at home. Two penalties and the opposition keeper sent off. Lucky buggers.

'Typical,' Dad says. 'It's all fixed, Davey. It's all a Suffolk conspiracy to stop Norwich from winning the league. Here, I bet that ref today was from Suffolk. What do you reckon? Have a look in the programme.'

I look on the back of the programme. 'Nah, he's from Barnsley, Dad.'

'That's what he says,' Dad laughs. 'But I'd like to see it written down on his birth certificate!'

I laugh. The lights up ahead change and the traffic starts to move. Dad's company car purrs down the street.

We cruise along the ring road. There isn't too much traffic. The clouds get darker and the rain gets a bit heavier. As we get round to the other side of Norwich, near the A47, near the retail parks, Dad looks at me.

'Fancy a quick trip to Maccie D's?' he says.

I smile back at him. I don't even need to answer. As if I'd ever say no to a burger.

'Don't tell your mother, though, will you?'

I put my hand on my heart. 'Scout's honour,' I say.

* * *

We sit down at a table near the window looking across to Pet Superstore, and scoff our burgers and chips.

But then Dad puts his burger down and leans in towards me. 'David,' he says. He's got his serious voice on. 'Have you spoken to Ollie much lately?'

I put my burger down. I shake my head. 'Not really.'

Dad has a worried expression on his face. He looks down at the table.

'Why, Dad?'

Dad sighs. He looks back up at me. 'I was just wondering,' he says.

Dad looks out of the window. He picks a couple of chips up and stuffs them in his mouth. He looks bothered. And I don't know what to say. I pick my burger up and take a bite.

'Hey, maybe we should go to Pet Superstore, Davey,' Dad says in his matey-jokey voice. 'We could get City a new striker, replace that donkey Lewis. Pick ourselves up a penalty-box predator! What d'you reckon?'

I smile. 'Yeah, why not? Couldn't be any worse than what they've already got.'

We sit there without saying a word for ages, stuffing food into our mouths, staring out of the window at the rain.

All of a sudden Dad springs to life, tidying his rubbish on to his tray. 'Come on then, Davey,' he says.

'Let's get moving or Mum'll guess that we paid Ronald McDonald a visit. If we're quick we might have time to nip into the pet shop and buy the ref a guide dog!'

Back in the car, Dad puts the radio on and pulls out of the parking space. We head for home. I sit in the passenger seat, staring out of the window at the industrial estates and then, when we get out of Norwich and into the countryside, at the soggy hedgerows, ploughed fields, pig pens and rusty tractors. And the whole time I'm sitting there I want to say something about Ollie, to ask Dad what's going on. But I can't think of the right thing to say. So I sit there quietly.

Sunday

Gary

'I'm going out,' I say. Not that there's any point in saying it. Mum's working this morning, went ages ago. And Dad'll be sleeping off the pub for ages yet. 'Come on, Patch,' I call.

Patch comes padding over, wagging his tail. I grab his lead and heave the front door open.

I let Patch off the lead. He trots along by my heels, sniffing the road and the grass and trees. We go to the end of the road, then turn right, out of the village. There are no cars about, so I walk down the middle of the road, towards Henry's farm. Patch keeps to the verge, going in and out of the hedge. He's got a scent of something. Probably a rabbit. When he was younger, me and Dad would bring Patch up to Henry's and shoot rabbits. Patch weren't ever much of a gun dog. He's too spoilt, that's what Dad said. He'd go and fetch the rabbit, but the greedy bugger sometimes wouldn't bring it back. He'd take it off somewhere. Dad would always give Patch a kick up the arsehole when he did that, but Patch never learned. He's too old now, though. And Dad ain't interested in shooting any more.

I walk as far as the gate. Patch ain't nowhere to be seen. So I climb up on to the gate and sit. He'll turn up in a bit. Always does.

The sky's grey today. Again. It's not that warm. But there's quite a wind. Might blow the cloud away later. Patch comes out of the hedge with his nose to the ground. You can hear him sniffing and snorting. He follows this trail that goes round and round, through the grass and out into the field. He's in his own little world. After about half a minute, he's miles away across the field. And after a minute, I can't see him no more.

So I sit there, on the metal gate. Thinking. About tomorrow. About going back to Wendham High School. Cos I don't want to. No way. Nothing's gonna be different. And now Knaggs'll be twice as bad as he was. You could tell from the way he just sat there outside Moore's office, smirking like it was all a joke.

Cos that's all it is to him. Bastard. I bet he managed to get off without being in any trouble. And I know why, I think. It was David Wright. Had to be. He went in there to talk to Mr Moore – I saw him. And I bet he told him that Knaggs didn't do nothing and I just hit him for no reason. I bet.

But I have to go back, don't I? I haven't got another option. There are no other schools for miles around, and there aren't any buses that go to them anyhow. And I'm too young not to go to school. I s'pose I could just run off. Just leave for good. Don't know where to. But at least I wouldn't have to go to school. I could find somewhere to sleep, scrounge some food, maybe get a job.

I sigh. I can't see Patch anywhere. I whistle for him. Nothing. I whistle again. Still nothing. So I jump down off the gate and walk across the field, through the long grass to find him.

MONDAY

Zoë

I can't eat breakfast this morning. Even the thought of food turns my stomach. So I stay in my room instead and stare at my uniform. I really don't want to go to a new school, simple as that.

At half seven, Mum comes up the stairs and knocks on my door. Gently. She opens it and peeps round the corner. 'Zoë, love, are you going to get ready for school? We've got to go soon.'

I make a face and sigh. 'I don't want to go, Mum,' I say. I don't want to cry, but I do.

Mum sits down on the bed, puts her arm round me and pulls me over towards her. 'Don't cry, Zo,' she says. 'You'll set me off.' I already have set her off – I can hear it in her voice. 'You'll be fine, Zoë,' she says. 'You've always been a confident girl. You'll make new friends easily. Anyway, you've already got a friend at the school, haven't you? Gary, isn't it?'

I sit up and nod. And then I sigh. 'I don't want to go to Wendham High School, though. I want to go back to my old school, with my old friends, Mum,' I say. 'I didn't want to move to this shithole.'

Mum sits up straight and looks at me. Her face is cross for a second. 'Zoë!' she says, like she's never heard me swear before. But then she just looks upset. 'I know it's a big change, Zoë. But Norfolk's a nice place. Much nicer than Morden. It'll be a great place for us to bring up the baby. And you. Just give it a chance.'

I look away from her.

'Listen,' she says. 'Why don't we treat ourselves this evening? We could go into town and get a DVD and a takeaway. Your choice. Indian, Chinese, fish and chips – whatever you want.'

I give her a smile. Just a little one, though. 'Can I choose the DVD?'

She smiles. 'Yeah, as long as you get dressed and go to school,' she says. Mum gets up from the bed. 'Leaving in fifteen minutes, Zoë. Make sure you're ready.'

And then she goes back downstairs.

* * *

The receptionist at school asks us to wait outside the office on some comfy chairs. Mum looks at me. She raises her eyebrows and smiles. I just sit there and feel uncomfortable in my new uniform.

After a couple of minutes, a tall man in a suit comes over to us. Mr Scott. Mum looks up at him and smiles. He shows us round the school and gives us all the talk about what a great school it is and how I'll love it here and how good the GCSE results are and blah-blah-blah. Mum laughs at all his jokes, like she's the new girl. She seems nervous. The school's a bit like Morden High School. Except it's much smaller. My form tutor's a man called Mr Sharkey. He has black and white hair. Makes him look a bit like a badger. Then we go back to the office and Mr Scott talks some more, but I've stopped listening. My heart's beating too fast to concentrate.

The school bell goes and Mum gets up to leave. And suddenly I feel about three years old. I want my mummy. She wishes me luck and blows me a kiss. And for a few seconds I really wish I could go with her. But then she's gone.

Mr Scott smiles at me. 'Don't worry, Zoë. Year Ten are a really nice year group. You'll settle in easily. And if you have any worries, you can always talk to Mr Sharkey or you can come and talk to me, OK?'

'Yeah,' I say. 'I'm a bit nervous, that's all.'

He smiles again. 'That's just natural, Zoë. You'll be fine. Let's go and meet Ten M, shall we?'

I nod and follow Mr Scott.

We walk down loads of corridors that all look the same. There's no way I'm gonna remember my way round this place. We stop by a door. Mr Scott smiles at me and then knocks. My hands are clammy. My stomach keeps turning. I feel like I'm gonna be sick. Mr Scott opens the classroom door and walks in. I stumble along behind him.

'Good morning, Ten M,' he says.

Ten M stand behind their chairs. 'Good morning, Mr Scott,' they say. And they all sit back down again.

Everyone looks at me. This is so embarrassing. I stand slightly behind Mr Scott, so they can't really see me.

'I'd like to introduce you all to Zoë,' he says. He steps aside, so that everyone can see me.

I smile at them. A couple of girls smile back, one even gives a little wave. Some of the boys smile back. But not many. Some of them look miserable, or don't look at all. And right at the back, in the corner, I see the two boys from the playing field – the one in the cap and his tall friend. They're smiling as they look over at me. But I can't tell if they're smiling cos they recognise me, or whether they're taking the piss again.

'Zoë is joining us from a school in London,' Mr Scott says, like everyone should be impressed. 'I'm sure that we're all going to make her feel welcome here at Wendham.'

A couple of the kids smile again. The two boys from the park say something to each other and then laugh. I think they're taking the piss.

Mr Sharkey shows me to my new seat, near the front of the class, opposite two boys who don't look up when I sit down. There's an empty seat next to mine. This doesn't look promising. I remember when new kids started at Morden, the teachers always gave someone the job of looking after them, helping them to settle in. All I get is an empty chair. Nice touch.

Mr Sharkey calls the register. I just concentrate on trying not to sound too stupid when I answer my name. Which I manage, just about.

When the register's done with, Mr Sharkey tells everyone to get a book out and read. He comes over and talks to me about my timetable. But I don't really hear what he's saying – I'm too busy trying to take everything in. Behind Mr Sharkey, I can see the rest of the tutor group. A lot of them are looking at me and talking. I just want to be at home. In Morden. I can't go through with this.

The bell goes. Most of the tutor group get up to leave.

Mr Sharkey – who's been crouching next to me –

stands up. 'Sit down, Ten M,' he says. 'You will go when I tell you it is time to go!'

Ten M roll their eyes, groan and sit back down.

'Put up your hand if you are in set one for science, please,' Mr Sharkey says. A few hands go up. Mr Sharkey looks at them. 'Paul, can you come over here, please?' he says. 'The rest of you, off you go to your lessons.'

The class chatter and leave the tutor room. Paul comes over to me and Mr Sharkey. I should have guessed who Paul would be: the boy in the cap from the playing field. Only now he isn't wearing the cap. He has long floppy blond hair instead. He kind of smirks at me as he walks over.

'Paul, I'd like you to take Zoë to science, please,' Mr Sharkey says.

Paul nods his floppy-haired head. 'Yes, sir,' he says. He seems all innocent and well behaved now. Maybe he was just being an arse in front of his friend. Some boys can be like that.

'Excellent,' Mr Sharkey says.

Paul smiles at Mr Sharkey. And we leave the classroom.

As soon as we're in the corridor, Paul turns to me. 'So, did you find him, then?' he says.

I look back at him. 'What?' I say. And then I think about it and realise I'm being thick. 'Oh, Gary. No. No, I didn't.'

'Why on earth were you looking for Gary Wood?'

I shrug. 'He's just a friend,' I say. 'I think.'

Paul gives me a look, like he doesn't understand me. 'You're friends with Gary Wood?'

I nod. 'Yeah, what's wrong with that?'

'He's a psycho, that's what.'

I look at Paul. He looks serious. 'He isn't,' I say. 'He's a bit quiet, but he isn't a psycho.'

Paul stops walking, so I do as well. 'Look at my face,' he says. 'You see this . . .' He points to the fading bruise on his cheek. 'That's where Wood hit me! For no reason. I'm telling you, he's a psycho. You should stay away from him. Seriously.' Paul starts walking again.

'He hit you? Why'd he hit you?'

Paul shrugs. 'No reason, like I said. He's just mental. They're sending him to see a shrink. Something's not right in his head!'

It starts to make sense now. Paul must be the boy who Gary hit, the reason he got excluded. I want to ask Paul about it, to find out why he did it, if Gary really is a psycho. But we've stopped in a little cloak-room outside the science labs. Paul hangs his stuff up. I do the same. He opens the door into a noisy science lab and we walk in.

David

I'm sitting in the science lab, feeling nervous, when Knaggs walks in. The bruise on the side of his face is a shiner. He's got a new girl with him. Looks like a bit of an indie girl. Blonde hair. Nice face. She's fit as well. And Knaggs has a huge grin on his face. Lucky sod. He's loving it. He takes her up to the front of the classroom, where Mr H is sitting. Knaggs stands behind the girl. He looks over at us and winks. Mr H smiles at the new girl and then starts talking to her. Knaggs doesn't come and sit down – he carries on standing behind the girl. He looks over at us again and smiles. And then he puts his hands just behind her, as though he's holding a pair of imaginary breasts. He blows a kiss and winks.

Everyone laughs.

Mr H stops talking to the new girl all of a sudden and looks around. Knaggs doesn't notice. He's now got his eyes closed, in an imaginary snog.

Everyone laughs again and Knaggs opens his eyes, stands up straight.

'Paul,' says Mr H, 'go and sit down. I will speak to you after the lesson.'

Knaggs comes and sits down at the bench, with a pissed-off look on his face. But as soon as he sits, the pissed-off look cracks into a grin.

'Who's that?' I ask.

'That, Davey-boy, is my future wife!' Knaggs says. 'Zoë.'

I look at her, standing at the front of the class, talking to Mr H. She looks amazing. I know she's only in her school uniform, but she looks good. 'She's nice,' I say. 'Where'd you find her?'

Knaggs shrugs. 'She's in my tutor group – Sharkey asked me to show her round,' he says. And then he blows a kiss towards her at the front of the classroom. She doesn't see it.

'Lucky you,' Joe says.

Knaggs smiles. 'Me and Millsy met her on Saturday, didn't we?'

Mills nods and smiles. 'Yeah.'

Knaggs leans in, like he's gonna tell us all a really big secret. 'She came up to us in the park and asked if we knew Gary.' He laughs.

'What, Gary Wood?' I ask.

Knaggs nods. 'Yeah, can you believe it?' And he laughs again.

'He kept quiet about *her*!' I say.

'I think if I was her, I'd be keeping quiet about *him*!' Knaggs says.

We laugh.

'She isn't really Wood's girlfriend, is she?' Joe asks.

Knaggs shrugs. 'Dunno. Doubt it. Why would someone like that even look twice at an ugly runt like Gary Wood?'

We nod. He's right.

Silence falls over our table for a few seconds. I look over at Wood's seat. It's empty. I heard a rumour earlier today that he was back in school. Apparently he was outside Mr Moore's office with his mum. He had a face like thunder, so I heard. But then, I suppose he would. To be honest, I'd prefer it if he didn't come back today. I don't really want to see him. Especially if he knows what I said to Mr Moore.

I turn back to Knaggs, Mills and Joe. 'Did you hear about Wood?' I say. 'Big Rob told me he saw him with his mum outside Moore's office!'

Mills and Joe shake their heads.

'I hope they've decided to kick him out for good,' Knaggs says. 'He's wrong in the head.'

We quieten down. Mr H is showing the new girl to her seat. There are only three empty seats in the classroom – Wood's seat, the seat next to Wood's and the seat next to Rachel Cluck. Mr H puts her in the seat next to Rachel. Rachel smiles at her.

Mr H starts the lesson by going through the homework. We have to mark in another colour. Mine isn't my finest effort – 17 out of 30. At least it's better than Knaggs's 12.

Mr H gathers us round the front of the lab to show us a DVD about gravity and space travel on the interactive whiteboard. Knaggs, me, Mills and Joe sit on the front bench. There's some crappy music at the start of the programme. We dance around the bench like mental cases. Who chooses the music for these things? Couldn't they choose something a bit less cheesy? It's hilarious. Then the voiceover on the video starts droning on about gravity and how rockets launch.

Knaggs taps me on the shoulder. And when I look round he hits me in the leg with the knuckle of his middle finger. I do the same back to him. Next shot, Knaggs manages to get me in the right spot and gives me a dead leg. I open my mouth and gasp in pain, try not to make a noise.

Mr H looks over. 'Um,' he says. 'Boys over there, if

you carry on messing about, I will switch off the DVD and you can make notes out of the textbook instead!'

We stop messing about. He's never done it before – switched off the DVD, that is – but we aren't gonna take the chance and end up having to copy out of a book. The programme drones on and on about gravity.

A few minutes later, the lab door opens. Mr Moore stands there and calls Mr Hambleton over. They talk for a few seconds. Mr Moore turns and leaves and then Mr H walks back into the classroom with Gary Wood. My heartbeat quickens. I feel nervous again. I watch him. He doesn't look at anyone as he walks in. He just goes over to his place, puts his pencil case down, grabs a stool near the front of the class to watch the DVD. I stare at him. I'm not sure if I want him to look up and see me or not. I don't know what I'd do – whether I'd smile at him, give him a sympathetic look, or just look away.

So I look at the DVD again. But I don't watch it.

And after a while, I get a poke in the ribs. Knaggs. He points over at Wood. 'He hasn't said hello to his girlfriend!' he whispers.

I pretend to laugh.

For the rest of the DVD, I keep turning to have a quick look at Wood, to see if he's looking at me. But he's just looking down, at the floor or something.

When it's finished, Mr H tells us to go back to our

places. Michael C hands out some textbooks, one between two. Paige hands out some photocopies of Mr H's handwritten questions about what was on the DVD.

'Use the textbook to help you with any questions you're not sure of,' he says.

I look over at Wood. He's still keeping his head down. I don't think he's said anything to anyone since he came into the lab. I don't think he's even looked at anyone. He's already writing something down. He has his textbook open in front of him. Then I look round at the new girl, Zoë. She's writing as well. But she keeps looking around, towards Wood. Maybe Knaggs is right. Maybe she is Wood's girlfriend.

I settle down, answer the first couple of questions by looking up the answers in the textbook. It's quiet in the lab. But after a couple of minutes, Knaggs whispers my name and then Mills's name. We look up at him. He points at Wood with a finger on his left hand and then at the new girl with a finger on his right hand. Then he brings the tips of his fingers together and makes them kiss.

We laugh.

He lays the finger of his right hand on the bench and puts the finger of his left hand on top. He makes the fingers hump each other.

We laugh again. But I stop. I feel guilty. I look over at Wood. Still working.

'Quiet!' calls Mr H.

So we're quiet. We just look at each other and giggle instead. All the while, Wood doesn't look up from his work. And all the while, the new girl keeps turning round to look at him.

As the lesson goes on, the noise level goes up. At first Mr H shushes us, but after a while he doesn't bother. Knaggs takes his chance.

'Oi, Wood,' he says. 'You didn't tell us you had a girlfriend.'

Wood doesn't look up. He concentrates really hard on his work.

'She's pretty fit actually,' Knaggs says. 'I wouldn't kick her out of bed for farting!' He laughs.

I look away for a second, as though I haven't heard him. I don't want to be a part of this. Not again. Wood's still sitting there, looking at his book. He's not writing any more, though.

'Hey, Wood,' Knaggs says.

Wood doesn't look up from his work.

'Does Zoë know that if she has kids with you, they'll be mixed race? Half human, half cheese puff!'

Wood looks up at the mention of Zoë's name. He looks at Knaggs. He looks like he did last week, angry as hell. 'Grow up, Knaggs,' he says. And he turns back to his work.

We all try to get on with our work again. All except

Knaggs. He looks over at Zoë on the other side of the lab and then at Wood.

'Zoë,' he says loudly, almost shouting.

I try to catch Knaggs's eye, to stop him. He ignores me.

Zoë turns round. So do most of the class.

'Did you know your new boyfriend is mental? Did you know he's got to go and get his head read by a shrink?'

Everyone looks at Zoë. She just sits there, her mouth open. She looks at Knaggs, then Wood, and finally Mr H.

'That's enough, Paul,' Mr H says. 'You will see me at the end of the lesson and you will explain yourself!'

And then, as everyone turns to look at Knaggs, to see his reaction, there's the sound of a stool being scraped backwards over the lab floor. Wood stands up. I expect him to come over and smack Knaggs in the face again. But he doesn't. He flings his pen down on to the bench and then marches out of the lab, without looking at anyone.

Zoë

The door shuts and Gary's gone. No one moves. No one does a thing. Not even the teacher. They all just sit there, looking at each other, looking at me, looking at the door. This isn't right. Someone's got to do something. I stand up, send my stool skidding back behind me. The classroom's silent. I can tell everyone's looking at me. I head towards the door.

'No, Zoë,' the teacher says. 'Stay here, please. Leave Gary be.'

I stop in my tracks, look at the teacher. For God's sake. This is unbelievable. I sigh. Someone has to go after him. I look over at Paul Knaggs. He's got a stupid bloody grin on his face. How can he? What an arsehole! I shake my head at him and he just smiles even wider.

I can feel myself going red now. Everyone's looking at me, like I'm weird. On my first day. I don't believe this. I must still be asleep. Please let this be a dream. A nightmare.

'Sit down, please, Zoë,' the teacher says.

I sigh. I go back to my stool and sit down. I want the floor to open up and swallow me.

He carries on with the rest of the lesson like nothing's happened, just like normal. Except it feels a bit weird in here. Tense. Everyone seems nervous. It's quiet. But I can tell that everyone is whispering about it, sniggering, looking over at me.

Rachel turns to me. 'Are you all right?'

I sigh. 'I dunno.'

I sit and wait for the lesson to end.

As soon as the bell goes, I get straight out of the lab, grab my stuff from the cloakroom and get out of the school building. Into the playground. Take great big lungfuls of air. I need it. I can't believe what's just happened. Could it possibly have been any worse? I'm in shock, I think. I don't know what to do. I want to just leave. Go home. Back to London.

I think about going and finding Gary. He seemed like he needed someone. It's his first day back. And it's all gone wrong again. But I don't even know where to begin. I don't know my way round the school. I've got no chance of finding someone who doesn't want to be found.

So I just walk round the playground instead. And Gary's not there. Just a load of kids, staring at me like I have some kind of disease. This is not good. This is very, very bad. I'm an outcast.

Gary

I knew it would be like this. The same as before. Knew it. I knew Paul Knaggs would be just the same as he was. I knew he'd take the mickey as soon as he saw me again. It's gonna be even worse than it was before. There's nothing that I can do about it. See, cos when Mr Moore found out about me hitting him the other day, Knaggs thinks that it was me grassing him up for taking the piss out of me. That's not how it happened. Mr Moore found me. In the corridor. He must have been able to tell that something was wrong, cos he took me into his office. And I didn't say nothing. It weren't till bloody Knaggs came in that he realised what happened. But Knaggs don't know that.

He thinks I just ran crying to Mr Moore. And now he's gonna make me pay.

And I don't know what I can do about it. I haven't got a clue. I can't go and tell anyone, can't go and tell Mr Moore. The teachers wouldn't do nothing anyway. They probably wouldn't believe me. They think I'm mad anyway. They want me to go and see a shrink. Maybe they're right. Maybe I am mad. Maybe that's why I couldn't handle it when Knaggs was saying all that shit. Maybe that's why I couldn't say nothing back to him, why I couldn't even think of nothing to say, why I just got angrier and angrier and had to hit something so I didn't explode.

I could hit Knaggs again. It's what Dad would tell me to do. And I'm stronger than Knaggs. I could punch him so hard he can't say nothing else ever again. So he can't even think nothing else. Except if I do that, I'll know I'm mad. They'll definitely make me go and see a shrink then. They'll bring a straitjacket for me and chuck me in the back of a van and take me away – to the loony bin or to the cops. Lock me up. You know, that's what Mr Moore said: 'You're lucky that we don't involve the police in this matter, Gary.'

And I know I can't just ignore it. Every time Knaggs says something, every time he looks at me with that smirk on his face, it makes my blood boil, my head ache. I can't help it. I can't ignore him. The only way to shut him up is to hit him. It's the only thing that works.

So maybe I just won't come in. Maybe I'll skive off school for the rest of my life. Put on a voice, phone up the school and say I'm ill or something. Cos I have to do something.

Zoë

The bell goes. End of my first day at Wendham High School. The worst day of my life. Probably. But I've survived it, just about. Even though everyone now probably thinks I'm some kind of weirdo. Rachel's sweet, though. She's got such a quiet voice, really nervous.

When we get out of the school, she shows me to the field, to wait for the coach back home. I walk over to where the other people from Wallingham are waiting. And I see him. For the first time since this morning, in science. Gary. He's standing there at the bus stop, with his head down. He looks pretty much suicidal. I stand there for a bit. Thinking. I've already made myself look like enough of a social retard for one day. Maybe I should just leave Gary there on his own, pretend like I haven't noticed him. Maybe he *is* just trouble. Maybe it was me that misunderstood him, not everyone else. But I can't do it. I can't ignore him. He's a human being. And besides, I can't really make myself look much worse than I already have. So I go over.

'All right?' I say.

He looks at the ground. He mumbles something. I can't make out whether it's 'yeah' or 'no' or 'hello'.

'I was looking for you earlier,' I say. 'After what happened in science.'

He looks up for a second, like he doesn't believe me. 'Really?'

I nod. 'Yeah. Didn't find you, though. Obviously!'

He doesn't say anything. He just stands there with his blazer hunched round his shoulders, his hands in his pockets.

'Are you OK?'

Gary shrugs his shoulders. He doesn't look all right. He looks like he wants to be anywhere but here. And I don't know what else to say to him. So we stand there in silence and wait for the coach.

It arrives a couple of minutes later. One of the teachers comes and leads us over to it. Up ahead, I see Paul Knaggs get on. He's got a cap on now. And he's taken his blazer and tie off. His shirt is untucked. He's got trainers on instead of shoes. Quite nice ones. Expensive ones. He thinks he's pretty special, you can tell.

Knaggs goes straight to the back of the bus. I wait for Gary to get on. He sits near the front, even though there are loads of seats further back up the bus. I sit next to him. He looks at me as I sit down.

'Do you mind if I sit here?'

He looks at me again. He shakes his head. 'Free country,' he says. And he turns to look out of the window.

We sit there in silence as the bus rattles along the tiny roads. There are fields on either side of the road, all the way back. Hardly any houses. And the bus drivers round here are even more psycho than the ones in Morden. They just speed along the country roads at about sixty miles an hour. So I try to look out of the side windows instead of out of the front.

Mum's in the lounge, on the sofa, when I get home. She's sipping a cup of tea and watching telly.

'Hi, love,' she says. 'How was it?'

I drop my bag on the floor by my feet. 'Not so good,' I say.

Mum's expression changes. She looks disappointed. 'Oh dear. What happened?'

I flop down on the sofa next to her. 'Everything just went really wrong,' I say. 'I think I've managed to make everybody think I'm a weirdo on my first day.'

Mum puts her cup of tea down on the floor and then puts her arm round me. 'Oh, Zo,' she says. 'I'm sure they don't think that really. You're just being paranoid.'

I look at her. 'No, seriously, Mum. They do think I'm weird!'

'Why would they think that?' Mum asks.

I sigh. 'It's just . . .' But I don't know what I'm trying to say. I sigh. 'They think Gary's my boyfriend.'

Mum makes a face, like, *'he had better not be your boyfriend, young lady'*.

'Relax, Mum, he's not my boyfriend! No way. It's just they were all picking on him and . . .'

Mum makes a sorrowful face and pulls me in for a hug. 'Don't worry about it, Zoë. They don't think you're weird, because you're not weird.'

I give Mum a smile.

'Do you want a cup of tea, love?' she says. 'It's only just made – there's one in the pot.'

I shake my head. 'No. I'm gonna go out for a bit. I need to sort my head out.'

'Haven't you got homework?' Mum asks.

I shake my head. 'They let me off today,' I say. Which is a lie.

Mum makes a face, like she's thinking about it. 'Well, OK,' she says. 'But make sure you change out of your uniform first.'

'Thanks, Mum,' I say. And I head out of the lounge and then the front door.

I walk out of the village, towards the farm first of all. The sky's clearing just as the sun's starting to go down. And it's getting cold. I climb over the gate, half walk, half run across the field and into the barn. Gary isn't there. Just the same collection of farm machinery, empty cider bottles, fag ends and dust.

I walk over to the farmhouse. It's too dark to see clearly, but I can't see Gary in there. Just loads more dust and a table that's got some empty bottles and a carrier bag on it.

So I walk back through the village, towards the playing field. And I see that tramp again. The medal man. He looks rough – in a bad way. His face looks really red. Purple almost. And he's got a cut on his face. It's bleeding. He's swaying all over the road, swinging a blue plastic carrier bag.

I stop in front of him. 'Are you all right?' I say.

The medal man doesn't look at me. He keeps swaying around. I don't think he knows I'm here. He's too out of it.

'Are you OK?'

This time, he kind of looks up. Stops walking. But

he still doesn't seem to see me. He stays really still for a second, as though he can hear a sound, like he's listening out for something.

'Do you need any help?' I ask.

He makes a confused face. Then an angry face. He mumbles to himself. And he starts walking again, swaying all over the place just like before, swinging the plastic bag.

I carry on walking as well. I kick a stone as I'm walking, till it hits a bump and flies up into the hedge. As I walk, I start to wonder whether I should go after him, the medal man. Get him to go and see a doctor or something. He looked bad. I turn round and look down the road. But he's gone. He'll be OK. I turn back and walk towards the village.

Gary isn't at the playing field, either. Hardly anyone is – just me, the man with the yappy dog and Paul Bloody Knaggs. As soon as I see it's him, I think about turning round and going straight home. But I think too slowly, cos he notices me, jumps off the swings and walks across the playing field towards me.

'You just can't keep away, can you?' he says.

I roll my eyes. And walk straight past him.

He follows me. 'Where's your boyfriend, then? Is he in a mood?'

I turn and give him a look. 'Grow up!' I say.

He sort of looks at me, like he's studying my face for clues. 'Oh, I get it,' he says. 'You were looking for lover boy, weren't you?'

I don't say anything. But I feel myself blush.

Knaggs smirks. 'I knew it.'

I quicken my pace to try and leave him behind. But Paul walks just as quickly.

'You know, Zoë, you could do much better than Wood. You're not all that bad-looking, in a certain light.'

I narrow my eyes at him and say nothing. I keep on walking, past the social club and out on to the gravel driveway.

'I don't understand what you see in him,' Paul says. 'The guy's a freak, a loser, a psycho. You saw it for yourself. Why bother with him?'

I stop walking, turn and look at him. 'If anyone's a freak, it's you!' I say. 'You're the one with the problem as far as I can see. You're the psycho that's been trying to make other people's lives a misery.'

He looks at me like he doesn't know what to say. For a second I think, *That's it, I've put him in his place.* But then he smirks.

'Why are you doing this?' I say. 'You must have some serious issues!'

He just stands there, that annoying smirk on his face. I want to hit him. I want to shake him, make him realise how much of an arse he's being. But I know that whatever I do, he's just gonna stand there, smirking like a little kid. So, I turn away and walk off towards the road.

'Slag!' he shouts after me.

David

We're at the dinner table. Pizza. And some salad out of a packet. Dad and Ollie are both scoffing their faces. Mum's just sitting there, though, thinking, staring into space.

'I was doing Margaret's appraisal today, David,' she says.

I nod. The pizza in my mouth is more difficult to chew all of a sudden. I don't look up, cos I know what she's gonna say next, what she's getting at.

'She said Gary went back to school today. She had to go and take him in and speak to Mr Moore.'

'Yeah,' I say. 'That's right.'

'Did you see him?' Mum says. She's looking straight

at me, I can tell. I try to meet her eyes for a second. Then I look away, down at my plate, cut some food.

'Yeah,' I say. 'Just in science, though.'

Mum nods. She cuts some pizza and puts it in her mouth. And I think I've got away lightly, if that's all she's gonna ask me about Wood. But then, when she's finished her mouthful, she looks at me again. 'Was he all right?' she says. 'Gary, I mean.'

I take a deep breath. My heart starts thumping. What's the right answer to this? How can I say that, no, he wasn't OK, cos my best mate gave him a hard time again? 'I'm not sure,' I say. 'He walked out of science. Not sure why . . .'

Mum puts her knife and fork down with a clunk on the table. 'Really?' she says, like she's shocked. 'Oh no. Why?'

I shake my head. 'I dunno,' I lie. 'Think he got upset about something.'

'Oh no,' Mum says. 'That's awful. Margaret'll be beside herself. She's really worried about him.'

It's quiet for a while. Mum picks up her knife and fork again. I try to eat some more of my pizza and salad.

'Good day today, Ollie?' Dad says, after a while.

Ollie shrugs. 'All right.'

'Right,' Dad says, and takes a sip of his tea. 'You

know, Ollie, maybe it's time to think about getting a proper job.'

There's the noise of knives and forks scraping plates and people chewing their food.

But Ollie has stopped eating. 'I *have* a proper job,' he says.

Dad stops eating and looks across the table at Ollie. 'OK,' he says. 'Fair point. But maybe you should start thinking about a career. Not a supermarket job. You could come and work for me. You'd have to start at the bottom, but a bright spark like you'd soon get promoted.' Dad smiles.

Ollie stares at Dad. 'I want to work in a supermarket, though. I like it. I don't want to sell chicken feeders to farmers, like you.'

'Not for the rest of your life, Ollie,' Dad says.

Ollie shrugs. 'Why not?'

Dad doesn't answer. He picks up his Norwich City mug and takes a gulp. He shakes his head, like he doesn't understand. 'You are joking?' he says.

Ollie bends over his plate again. He doesn't answer.

'Maybe you should think about going back to college, then,' Dad says.

Ollie sighs really loudly. He picks up his pizza in his hands and ignores Dad.

'No?' Dad says.

Ollie shrugs. He chews his pizza.

'Maybe we should have this conversation another time,' Mum says.

Dad shakes his head again and attacks the lettuce leaves on his plate with his fork.

There's silence. No one wants to say anything. There's an atmosphere. I look out of the kitchen window while I'm eating, so I don't have to look at anyone.

Mum breaks the silence. 'Could you keep an eye on Gary for me?'

I stop in mid-chew. I'm not sure what to say. I can't say no, I suppose. But I don't want to say yes.

'Please,' she says. 'You always used to play together when you were babies. Just keep an eye on him, that's all.'

I look at Mum. 'S'pose,' I say.

'It would mean a lot to me, David. Margaret's at the end of her tether over all this. She's not sure what to do . . .'

I nod. 'OK.' And then I look back at my plate, spear a bit of lettuce and eat it.

Zoë

I did something weird tonight – a bit stalkery. After I got back from the playing field. I got the phone book out and looked 'Wood' up in it. Wasn't hard to find his number. There were thousands of 'Woods' listed in Norfolk. But only one 'Wood'. In Wallingham. *Wood, R.* It has to be his number.

I thought about ringing. I even got as far as picking up my phone. But then I realised I didn't know what I'd say. And besides, like I said, it would look like I was stalking him. I saved the number in my mobile, though, and I wrote the address down. Just in case.

Gary

I used to help Dad on the farm a lot. Sometimes we'd move the cows from field to field. Henry's farm was so spread out – he had fields all round Wallingham – that sometimes we'd shift the cows quite a long way and we'd have to walk them along the roads. Dad would get me to hold the gates open for him. Don't sound like a very responsible job, but it was. See, if you don't hold the gate properly, so it closes off one part of the road, the cows'll end up going the wrong way and causing havoc on the roads. That happened once, when I was holding the gate – I left a little gap and a young Friesian squeezed past and ran off the wrong way down the road. It took them hours to get her back. But they did.

I must've only been about seven or eight, but Henry got really angry with me – started yelling and swearing his head off. Dad stood up for me when Henry started yelling. He got right in Henry's face and told him that if he wanted his bloody cows looking after, he should shut his stupid gob. Told him to stick his crappy job up his lazy arse. I was scared. I thought they were gonna have a fight. I thought Dad was gonna lose his job. And it would all have been my fault. But Henry just walked away.

And after a while Dad calmed down too. Mum made him go back into work the next day and say sorry. I think Henry grumbled a bit, but he let Dad come back all the same. Probably cos otherwise he'd have had to get off his lazy arse and do some work for himself.

TUESDAY

Zoë

'Come on, Zoë, get up,' Mum says. She opens my bedroom door and walks in. 'Time to get up for school.'

I sigh and roll over. I pull the pillow over my head. I just want to block the day out. I want to go to sleep and wake up somewhere else, so I don't have to get up and go to Wendham High School.

'Come on,' Mum says. She puts her hand on my shoulder and gives me a gentle shake.

I sigh again.

Mum gently lifts the pillow off my head. I look up at her. 'Oh, you are in there,' she says, smiling.

I don't smile back.

'Time to get up, love. Otherwise you'll be late for school.'

I sit up in bed. 'I'm not feeling well,' I say. 'I can't go to school today. I've got a stomach ache.'

'Really?'

I nod my head.

'Let me feel your temperature,' Mum says. And she puts her cold hand on my forehead. 'You don't feel hot.'

I look up at Mum. I used to be able to do this really well, when I didn't want to go into school. She'd always believe me. But I can tell from her face that she's not taken in this time.

She smiles. 'Why don't you come and have some breakfast?' she says. 'Might make you feel better. You've probably just got second-day nerves, Zoë.'

Mum goes back out of my bedroom and down the stairs. I sit on my bed. I reach over to my bedside table and grab my white T-shirt. I took it into school last Tuesday, my last day at Morden High. I took a marker pen as well. All my friends signed it and wrote messages. I start reading them again. It's weird. It seems like a year ago now, since I was there. It seems like a different lifetime. Seems like a different Zoë.

David

PE. The changing rooms. It's mental in here sometimes. Mainly cos Mr Lawson never comes in and checks that we're behaving ourselves – he just leaves us on our own. To do our own thing. Anyone who's got any sense gets changed as quick as they can and then goes straight into the gym, so they stay out of the mickey-taking and stuff. That's what all the pebbleheads like Gary Wood do. Cos they know that otherwise they'll end up getting the piss taken out of them.

I'm nearly changed myself. I've got my T-shirt and shorts on. I just need to put my trainers on. Next to me, Knaggs is still in his school uniform, though. He's only taken his tie off so far. He's spent the rest of the time taking the mick out of people, prowling around the changing rooms. It always makes me feel nervous being in here, in case someone starts taking the mick out of me. Although with Knaggs around I guess they won't.

'Hey, Davey,' Knaggs says. 'Watch this.' He walks over to the corner of the changing rooms – the corner reserved for pebbleheads.

'What you doing?' I say.

Knaggs grins at me. He takes a bag off the bench and holds it out for me to see. 'This is Wood's bag, isn't it?'

I look at it. It's a skanky old black rucksack with holes in it. 'Think so. Yeah. Why?'

Knaggs grins again. He opens the drawstring at the top of the bag and looks inside. After a few seconds he pulls out a lunch box. 'Well, lookee here,' he says. 'Farmer Boy's got ham sandwiches for his lunch!' He takes a sandwich out of the lunch box and takes a bite. Then he makes a face. 'Oh, yuck,' he says. 'That's disgusting.' He stops chewing and lets the half-chewed sandwich fall out of his mouth.

I'm not the only person watching. There are about five or six of us left in the changing rooms. We're all looking at Knaggs and laughing kind of nervously.

Knaggs puts the lid back on the lunch box and tosses

it away. It slides across the changing-room floor till it hits the wall and stops. Knaggs has another look in the bag. This time he pulls out a pencil case and throws it across the floor after the lunch box. We laugh again. He looks in the bag, has a good rummage around. And after a few seconds he pulls a bottle out of Wood's bag. He looks at us and smiles. We all laugh again. Knaggs unscrews the lid. He takes a sniff of the drink.

'Lemon squash!' he says. 'My favourite!' He has another sniff. 'Ah, a good vintage as well.' He takes a swig. He swills it around his mouth, like he's a wine taster or something, then spits it out all over the changing-room floor.

No one is changing any more – we're all looking at Knaggs, wondering what he'll do next.

'Not bad,' he says, gazing into the distance like he's thinking of the best way to describe a wine. 'Quite fruity, but it could do with something else. A bit more body, I think.'

We laugh again.

Knaggs stops and smiles back at his audience before he continues. 'This should sort it,' he says. And he makes a noise in the back of his throat, trying to cough up a greenie. He holds the bottle below his mouth and then opens his lips. A stringy, luminous greenie starts to leak from Knaggs's mouth. It stretches down, really slowly. Until it lands, plop, in Wood's drink.

'Eeeuuurrrggghhh!' we all say.

Knaggs looks up. He smiles and gives us a wink. And then he screws the lid back on to Wood's bottle and puts it back into the bag.

PE was circuit training. I think Mr Lawson must have been getting his own back after the football lesson the other day when we all walked off, cos it was knackering in there today. I go straight to my peg and open my bag. I'm thirsty as hell. I get my water bottle out and take the lid off. But before I can take a sip, I get a nudge. I turn round.

'Have you checked that bottle for any, erm, bits?' Knaggs says. He smirks.

My stomach turns. I remember Wood's bottle and Knaggs's stringy greenie. I screw the lid on to my bottle and put it into my bag. I think I'll drink from the water fountain today.

'What's up, Davey?' Knaggs says. 'You not thirsty?' He reaches into his own bag and grabs his bottle. He takes a big, long swig of it, wipes his mouth with his arm and grins at me.

I start getting changed out of my PE kit. I'm sweaty as anything. But there's no way I'm having a shower. Mr Lawson used to force us to have showers back in year seven. But no one does any more. So I use my T-shirt to wipe up all the sweat and then give myself a good spray with deodorant. As I'm putting the lid back on my deodorant, Knaggs gives me another nudge.

'Look,' he says.

I look behind me. Wood walks through the changing rooms with his head down. He walks over to the bench and sits. The changing rooms go quiet. It seems like everyone's looking at Wood. He opens the draw-string at the top of his bag and looks inside. He can tell straight away that someone's been messing with his stuff. But he doesn't say anything. He just looks around for his lunch box and then for his pencil case and puts them back in his bag.

I look at Knaggs. He's got a massive grin on his face.

Wood sits on the bench again. He looks in his bag again and then pulls out his drink bottle. Knaggs gives me another nudge. My stomach turns over again. I feel like I want to be sick. I should say something now. I should stop Wood before he takes a swig. But my mouth won't open. I can't. Not with everyone watching. Wood lifts the bottle to his mouth. He gulps it down thirstily. I have to look away. I look at Knaggs instead. He's watching Wood with a massive grin on his face.

Lunchtime. We're in the playground, having a kick-about with a tennis ball. There are about ten of us playing Wembley. Joe's in goal. The rest of us are playing, all against all. Knaggs is the first one to score. A tap in on the line, after Dougie's been on a long run. That's what Knaggs always does. He's a complete goal hanger.

Dougie's next through, with a screamer of a shot. He does a lap of honour before he goes and stands behind the goal with Knaggs.

Joe kicks the ball out again. Mills controls the ball and takes a couple of people on. He goes past them and then takes a shot at the goal. Joe sticks out a foot and the ball rebounds off it, straight to me. I control it. Swing my left leg.

GOAL!!

I raise my hand in celebration and then go and stand behind the goal with Dougie and Knaggs. We watch the others running around after the tennis ball.

But something else catches my eye. Wood. He comes out of the double doors from the school building. He doesn't notice us. He just starts walking across the playground, head down.

'You looking at what I'm looking at?' Knaggs says.

I don't answer him.

'Watch this . . .' he says. And he walks over to Wood. 'Hey, Gary,' he says.

Wood looks up at Knaggs.

'That was a tiring PE lesson, wasn't it?'

Wood doesn't answer him. He just stares at Knaggs,

like he doesn't trust him.

'Don't know about you, but I needed a good long drink after that, didn't you?'

Wood still doesn't answer. He just looks at Knaggs like he doesn't understand.

'What drink did you have today?' Knaggs says.

Wood just stares back at him.

'Lemon squash, wasn't it?'

Wood looks away from Knaggs, down at his shoes.

'Did it have bits in it?'

Wood looks back up at Knaggs. He's going red. 'Shut up.'

'Just asking,' Knaggs says. Then he smirks. 'Cos I flobbed in someone's drink earlier. By mistake, of course. Thought it might have been yours. Was it a bit stringy? A bit flobby?'

Wood stares at Knaggs. Knaggs just smirks. And then Wood starts to look all pale and clammy. His cheeks puff out. His eyes bulge. And then his mouth opens and he chucks up everywhere.

And I'm standing here, just staring. Next to me, Knaggs starts wetting himself laughing. So does Dougie. But I can't. I watch Wood as he walks away and I feel guilty. I should have stopped Knaggs.

Zoë

When school finishes and we all go to the field to get the bus, I see Gary. He's on his own, staring silently at the ground again.

'Hi, Gary,' I say.

He sighs and says nothing.

I sit next to him on the bus anyway. He doesn't say a word to me. He sits there and stares out of the window. He looks really angry and fed up. Kind of like how I feel.

As soon as the bus stops in Wallingham, Gary takes off without saying anything. He's round the corner and out of sight before most people are off the bus. Something must have happened today. I don't know whether to go after Gary or to leave him. But as I'm standing at the bus stop, wondering what to do, Paul Knaggs comes swaggering over towards me.

'He looked angry, Zoë,' he says. 'I wonder what all that was about?'

I stare at Knaggs. He has a smile on his face. He knows exactly what's happened to Gary. 'What have you done to him?'

Knaggs makes an innocent face. He pretends to be hurt that I could think he's done anything. Then he smiles again. 'What? Me? I didn't do anything to him. I just topped up his drink bottle for him, that's all!'

I have no idea what he means by that. But the smirk on his face says enough. 'You're such a pig!' I say. 'What's he ever done to you?'

Knaggs lifts his cap up ever so slightly and points at the bruise on his cheekbone that's beginning to fade. 'Well, duh!' he says. 'That was completely unprovoked!'

I don't believe a word of it.

'I'm telling you, Zoë,' he says. 'The guy's a psycho! When are you gonna listen?'

I turn to go.

'I s'pose you're gonna go and kiss him better, are you?' Knaggs says.

I walk off, towards the farm.

Gary's there, in the barn. He's not on the tractor,

though. He's on the floor, leaning against the wall. He's sitting with his head buried between his knees and his hands on the top of his head. His bag's next to him, on its side. The pile of cider bottles is still there, where I tidied them the other day, but now there are more bottles scattered around. I put my school bag down and sit next to Gary on the floor. I look at him for a few seconds, in silence.

'You all right, Gary?' I say. It's a stupid question. I only need to glance at him to realise he's pretty far from OK.

He doesn't answer. He just sighs and runs his hands through his hair.

'I had a crappy day today, as well,' I say. 'I officially hate Wendham High School.'

I look over at Gary. He doesn't say anything. He grits his teeth. I think he's crying, but he's not making a noise.

'Everyone thinks I'm weird,' I say. 'It's horrible. Everyone's avoiding me. I think they're all talking about me behind my back.'

Gary still doesn't look up, doesn't say anything.

'I don't know what to do about it,' I say. 'It wasn't like this at my last school. I used to have loads of friends . . . What do you think I should do?'

Gary lets out another sigh. He takes his head out from between his legs and looks at me. 'I don't know,' he says. 'Go back to wherever you came from. Stop hanging around with me! Leave me alone.'

His face is red and tense and angry. He stands up. He looks around the barn, spots the plastic bottles and marches over to them. With a swing of his right leg, he smacks three of them into the air. They land with a hollow thud. He looks around again, sees the bucket and kicks it across the barn. Then he kicks a box too. I feel a bit scared.

'Gary, please, don't,' I say. I sound feeble.

He ignores me, walks over to the big back wheel of the tractor and kicks it hard. It hardly makes a noise, doesn't move, but I think he's hurt his foot cos he winces.

'Are you all right?'

Gary nods and then takes a deep breath. He leans against the tractor.

'Did something happen today?'

Gary nods.

'What?'

He doesn't answer. He climbs up on to the tractor and sighs again.

'You can tell me,' I say. 'You don't need to be so angry with me. I didn't do anything.'

He looks at me. He kind of half smiles, I think, but it's gone in a fraction of a second. 'I don't want to talk about it,' he says. 'Leave it.'

So we don't talk about it, we leave it. Gary sits there, on the tractor, and stares at nothing. And I walk around the barn, thinking that maybe he's right, maybe I should just leave him here. Maybe I should pretend I never met him, as if I don't like him.

I pick the bucket up and put it back where it was and then I do the same with the box and the bottles. I go and stand near the entrance to the barn and I lean against the wall. I stare at the farmhouse. It looks different from last time. The door's open a bit, like it's been kicked in. For a second, I wonder if Gary did it. But then I think about what he said – about the farmer's family and how we shouldn't go in there. I don't think he'd have done something like that. Not even when he was angry.

'Have you seen that door?' I say. I turn to look at him.

'What?' he says.

'The farmhouse. Look, the door's been kicked in.'

Gary jumps down from the tractor and walks over towards me. He wipes his face and stares at the door. 'Someone's been in there,' he says. He carries on walking, past me, towards the farmhouse. 'Come on,' he says.

Gary disappears into the darkness of the house. I look around outside, check no one's looking. There's no one around – we're probably a mile away from the nearest human being. So I grab the door and follow him into the house. And straight away the smell hits me. I don't know what it smells like, but it's not very nice. Kind of sharp and stale, rank and meaty. I cover my nose and mouth with the sleeve of my blazer and carry on walking.

It's gloomy inside. I have to really peer at things to make out what they are. This room's a kitchen. There's a big table near the window, the one covered in dust and empty bottles. Gary stops and looks at it.

'Someone's definitely been in here,' he says. 'Look.' He points at the bottles.

'Who do you think left them here?'

Gary shrugs. 'Dunno.'

'Other kids?' I say.

Gary shakes his head. 'Doubt it,' he says. 'They all get pissed up in the churchyard.'

'Then who?' I say. 'The farmer's family?'

He shakes his head again. 'Why would they have forced the door?' He steps back from the table. 'I'm gonna have a look upstairs.' And he marches up the steps.

For a second I think about following Gary upstairs. I don't want to be down here on my own. I've seen horror films. I know what happens when people split up to look round old houses. But when I look up the stairs, I can't see where Gary's gone. And it looks even darker up there than it is down here. So I start having a look round the downstairs instead.

The kitchen's really scuzzy. The old sink is stained and looks like it might fall off the wall if anyone turns the tap on. And the little electric cooker is the old kind, like in my grandma's house, but filthy. Brown-stained, flower-patterned wallpaper hangs off the walls. It looks like the sort of kitchen that an old man has used. That sounds sexist, doesn't it? But I can't imagine a woman in this kitchen. Henry must have lived alone.

On the wall near the stairs there's a box. It has *KEYS* on it in faded lettering. There are two sets inside. One has a fob on it. I take them from the box. The fob has a badge on it. *DB*, it says. I recognise the badge – it's the same one as on the front of the tractor in the barn.

Then there's a noise, a rumbling, coming from upstairs, like someone falling over. I take a step to my left and look up the stairs, into the darkness.

'Are you all right, Gary?' I shout.

There's no answer. Just another rumble.

'Gary?'

Still no answer.

I grab the rail and start to climb the stairs slowly, staring into the dark. And straight away I realise that the bad smell's coming from upstairs, cos with each step the smell gets almost unbearable.

'Gary?' I say again. 'Are you OK? Where are you?'

It's silent for a few seconds. Then there's a voice. 'In here.' Gary's voice. Only flat.

I climb the rest of the stairs quickly. And then to my right, I see Gary standing in the doorway of a room, looking into it.

'Anything up here?'

Gary doesn't look round. He's got his hand over his mouth. He nods his head slowly. 'You shouldn't look,' he says.

I walk towards Gary. 'Why? What is it?'

As I get closer to him, the smell gets stronger. It's foul. I put my hand over my mouth and nose.

'Medal man,' Gary says. He turns to me with a solemn face.

'Is he all right?'

Gary shakes his head. 'He's dead.'

'What? Are you sure?' I say.

I push past Gary. And then I wish I hadn't. Because there he is, the medal man, lying on his side on the bed, covered in sick, purple in the face. There are more bottles scattered round the bed, and some cans too. And a blue plastic bag. The smell's disgusting. I retch and run out of the room.

'Oh my God!'

Gary sighs. 'Let's go downstairs,' he says. His voice sounds really flat. Sad.

We walk down the stairs, me covering my mouth, trying not to be sick, Gary holding my arm. He leads me to the kitchen table and pulls out a chair for me to sit on. I put my face in my hands and try to take some deep breaths, to get that smell out of my lungs, to get the picture of the purple face out of my brain. Gary doesn't sit down. I can sense him standing over me, looking at me, not knowing what to do.

'Do you want a drink of water or something?' he says.

I shake my head. I don't want anything out of this kitchen, out of this house. I just want to go. I take my hands away from my face. 'Can we go outside?'

Gary nods.

We leave the house. Me first, almost running, and Gary behind.

'Jesus!' he says. 'What shall we do?'

I take a couple more deep breaths. But I still feel sick. I keep seeing the medal man's purple face and that blue bag. I know I could have done something. 'We should call the police, I suppose.'

And then I retch. I throw up in the grass, crouch over and spit it out. Try and get rid of the smell from that room, of the picture in my head. And I retch again. I think I'm gonna be sick again. Deep breaths.

Breathe in. Breathe out. Let it pass.

Gary puts his hand gently on my arm and leads me a few steps away from the house. 'Have you got a phone?' he asks.

'In my bag,' I say. 'Over in the barn.'

The police and ambulance take ages to turn up. And when they do, it's like none of it's really happening. Like it's in a film and I'm just watching it. They go and check the body first of all, and tell us what we already know: he's dead. Died from choking on his own vomit, they say. Then they start to give us a lecture, about trespassing and stuff. I can't really take on board what they're saying. All I can think about is the body lying there. And the fact that I could have saved him yesterday, if only I'd gone and found him. Or told someone. Anything. And the smell. Sharp and stale and . . . oh, I can't think about it any more.

Halfway through the lecture, the policeman looks at me and stops talking. 'I think you should get home,' he says. 'Are your parents at home?'

I nod. 'Mum is.'

'I'll run you home,' he says. 'You've had a nasty shock.'

Like I don't know that already.

He drives us home in the police car, me and Gary. We stop outside my house first. The policeman gets out of the car and lets me out. But instead of getting back in the car, he walks me up to the door and then knocks.

Mum answers the door with a look of total horror.

'Zoë!' she says. 'What's happened? Where have you been?'

I look down at the ground.

'It's nothing to worry about, Mrs Wildsmith,' the policeman says. 'Zoë isn't in any trouble. She's just had a nasty shock.'

Mum gasps and throws her arms round me.

While the policeman explains what's happened, I get sent upstairs, 'to have a lie down'. Downstairs, I can hear Mum and the policeman talking. I stand by the door, just inside my room, and listen, but they're talking in hushed voices. All I catch is something about trespassing and dangerous buildings, then signs to look out for and counselling. The front door closes and Mum starts to walk up the stairs. I get into bed and pull the duvet up over myself.

A few seconds later, Mum knocks gently on my bedroom door and then opens it. She peers round the door. 'Mind if I come in?' she says in a gentle voice.

'No,' I say. It comes out in a croak.

Mum walks in and sits down on the end of my bed. 'You all right, love?'

I nod. But I don't feel all right. I feel strange.

Restless. I can't really explain it.

'Listen, love, if you need to talk about what you saw today, I just want you to know – you can talk to me. OK?'

I nod.

Mum looks at me. She has a sort of sad smile on her face. 'Would you like a hot chocolate or something?'

I shake my head. 'I'm all right, Mum. I just want to be on my own.'

When Mum's gone, I lie down on my bed. Only when I do, I can feel something in the pocket. The keys. I take them out of my pocket. Oh crap!

David

I'm up in my room, doing some maths homework, when I hear Mum's car crunch up the gravel in the drive. A minute or so later, she puts her key in the front door and comes into the house. I'm stuck on question seven, so I go downstairs.

'Hi, David,' she says. 'Ollie not at home?'

I shake my head.

'Ooh, what a day I've had. I'm cream-crackered,' Mum says. 'Be a love and put the kettle on, will you?'

I go through to the kitchen and grab the kettle.

'How was your day?' Mum calls through from the hallway.

I think for a second about Gary Wood. 'All right, bit

boring,' I say. Cos I can't mention the crap job I did of looking out for him today. How I let my best mate get away with flobbing in Gary's drink and how I watched him drink it. So I walk over to the sink and fill the kettle with water instead.

Mum walks into the kitchen, flicking through a wad of post. 'Bills, bills and more bills.'

I plug the kettle in and turn to Mum. 'Do you want tea?'

'Yeah,' she says.

I grab the box of tea bags out of the cupboard.

'Oh, make us a proper cup in the pot, will you?'

'OK,' I say. But what I really want to say to her is about what happened today, about Wood and Knaggs and the lemon squash. 'Mum?' I say.

'Yeah,' she says, looking at one of the bills.

I sigh. I can't say it. How would I say it? Maybe, '*Mum, you'll never guess how much of a coward I was today*.' I turn away from her to the cupboard and take down the tea pot and tea.

Gary

Dad used to moan like crazy about Henry. Mainly cos Henry was a lazy sod. Dad used to say that Henry couldn't be bothered to run a fucking bath, let alone a farm. I reckon if you didn't know the two of them, you'd think that Dad and Henry didn't get on. But they did.

Most nights they'd go down the Swan together. They used to sit at the bar and drink Guinness. Dad always said that Henry was a mean bastard as well as a lazy one – he'd never get Dad a drink. Dad reckoned Henry had this little scam going on in the pub. See, Henry'd buy a pint and drink about three quarters of it, so there was only a little bit left. Then he'd take it back to the bar and ask George, the landlord, to put another half in. George'd just fill it right up to the top again. After four pints, Henry'd got one free. He might have been lazy and mean but he wasn't stupid, old Henry.

It was Dad who found Henry's body. In the farmhouse. Dad wasn't working for him any more by then, but every so often he'd go and see Henry, check he was all right. Only that time he wasn't. He'd shot himself. Henry's family told everyone he'd been cleaning a gun, his finger had slipped and it was an accident. But I know that's not true. Even Henry weren't daft enough to clean a loaded shotgun that was pointed in his mouth. Poor bugger shot himself on purpose. He couldn't take it no more.

WEDNESDAY

Zoë

Mum looks at me, all concerned, as I walk into the kitchen. 'How are you feeling this morning?'

I sit down at the table. 'All right, I s'pose.'

But I don't feel all right. I'm lying. I feel weird. Tired. Guilty. I couldn't shut my eyes last night, cos every time I did I could see the medal man lying in that bed, covered in his own sick, purple, lifeless. I've never seen a dead body before. I had that horrible smell in my nostrils. And I kept playing those few seconds when I saw him staggering down the road the other day, when I thought about helping him, over and over in my head. I wish I'd done something different. I should have got him to go to a doctor. He'd be alive now. He'd be in hospital or a hostel. Instead of dead.

And when I wasn't thinking about the medal man, I was thinking about the tractor keys. By two in the morning I was so paranoid I was sure the police were gonna break down my door and search my bedroom. They'd have found the keys and done me for theft. Or murder. Or both. Last time I checked my clock, it said 03:10. I must have fallen asleep after that. The light was still on when I woke up.

'You should stay off school today, Zo,' Dad says. 'After what happened yesterday.'

I stare at him. I don't think I've ever heard Dad say I should stay off school before. He's usually the one saying I should go in, even if I'm dying of flu. He has a concerned look on his face.

'Really, Zoë,' he says. 'I think you should.'

I can't think straight and I'm so tired that I just nod my head.

'I'll phone the school,' Mum says.

David

I'm in my room, getting ready for school, when my phone goes. I pick it up off my bed and open the message. It's from Knaggs: **U will not believe this – Wood & Zoë found a dead tramp last night! Lol ;o)** I read it a couple of times to check whether I've missed something. I'm not sure if I'm meant to take it seriously or not. Maybe it's Knaggs's idea of a joke. I decide to try and ignore it. I put my phone down and finish doing my school tie up.

But I can't ignore it. I have to know what he means. So I pick up my phone again and text Knaggs back: **What? Is that a joke?**

I sit on my bed and wait for a reply. Twenty seconds

later my phone beeps again. **No. Serious! Big Rob's dad had to give them a lift home! They found it in Wallingham.**

Which makes sense, I s'pose, cos Big Rob's dad is a policeman. But what doesn't make sense is how they found a tramp's body. Or why they found a tramp's body. This is weird. I think about texting Knaggs back again, asking him for more details. But I put my blazer on and then go downstairs to get my bag for school.

Knaggs can't help himself. As soon as he sees Wood in the playground, he calls over to him, 'Oi, Wood. What's it like to kill a man?'

Wood looks up at him, confused. Only for a second, though. Cos then he gets his head down again, as though he's trying hard to ignore Knaggs. Knaggs walks closer to him, laughing.

'You gonna do a bag lady next, then?' Knaggs says.

Wood doesn't look up at all. He's trying not to react.

And I know what I should do. I should get Knaggs away from him. 'Knaggs,' I say.

But Knaggs ignores me, doesn't even look at me. He just follows Wood. 'Where's your girlfriend today?' he asks.

'Knaggs,' I say, 'come on, let's go –'

But Knaggs still doesn't look at me. He keeps following Wood. 'Oi, Wood,' he says. He sounds kind of angry, like he's trying to start a fight. 'I said, where's your girlfriend today?'

Wood looks angry too. He keeps walking towards the school building, away from Knaggs. But Knaggs keeps following.

'I heard she got sent to prison,' Knaggs says. 'Is it true?'

Wood's face is red now. He looks like he's gonna blow at any second. Knaggs should be careful. When Wood loses it he's scary.

'Knaggs,' I say, 'come on, let's go and play football.' I put my hand on Knaggs's arm. But he shrugs it straight off.

'Hey, I heard that the police were outside Mr Moore's office,' Knaggs says. 'They're on to you, Wood. You better start running.'

Wood doesn't look up. He's nearly at the doors now. He looks like he's either gonna cry or explode if he doesn't get away from Knaggs.

'You'll get life for killing a tramp,' Knaggs says. 'Hey, you better be careful in the prison showers!'

Wood reaches the doors into school. He pulls them open but then stops. He glares at Knaggs, like he's deciding whether to smack him in the face. And he stares at me, just for a second. Then he's gone.

Knaggs turns to me and smiles. 'Stupid bloody farmer,' he says.

Zoë

I've been up in my bedroom all morning. It's looking more like my room now with all my stuff scattered across the floor, untidy. You can hardly see the carpet. Mum usually complains about it, but she hasn't today. I wonder how long it'll last, this sympathy. I'm not sure whether I like it.

I keep looking at the keys. I need to get rid of them. I need to take them to the farmhouse. Maybe that's what I should do today: just take them there, put them back and then never go to the place again. Forget it happened. Forget about the medal man. Start my normal life in Norfolk right now. No more loners, no more psycho boys, no more dead tramps. Just normal people and normal things.

But I keep thinking about him. The medal man. It's really sad. That sounds like a really stupid thing to say, like an understatement, but what else do you say? Imagine that being how your life ends. Full of cider, choking on your own vomit in an abandoned farmhouse in the middle of nowhere. Poor guy. He must have a family somewhere, maybe brothers or sisters. He might have had kids. I wonder if they even know what's happened.

David

We're having science in the ICT room today. A bit of a novelty. Mr Hambleton wants us to make a Powerpoint presentation about space travel and gravity.

'Use some of the websites I'm writing on the board to help you with your research,' Mr H says. 'I want the first two slides done before lunchtime, please.'

And he lets us get on with it. We're all partnered up. All apart from Gary Wood. I'm working with Knaggs. Knaggs is on the right-hand side. He always sits there so he can be in control of the mouse. Same every lesson.

'Shall we start researching, then?' I say.

'Yeah,' Knaggs says. 'I have got something I want to research, as it happens!' He goes straight to Google and types in 'tramp murderer'.

'Knaggs, don't,' I say. And I try to grab the mouse off him.

But he just holds it away from me and presses 'search'.

I sigh and let him do it, hoping that he'll get bored in a moment so we can get our work done.

The results appear on-screen. Knaggs clicks on the top link. It's a news story on the BBC website about a man who set a tramp on fire while he was sleeping on a park bench.

'Jesus, look at him!' Knaggs says, pointing at the picture of the murderer. 'Look familiar?'

I stare at the picture. He does look familiar. He looks like Gary Wood, only about 20 years older. Same short ginger hair, same freckles, same half-angry, half-gormless look on his face. I laugh. 'Yeah!'

Knaggs right-clicks on the picture and copies it. He opens up a Powerpoint file and pastes the picture on to the first slide.

'Knaggs, don't,' I say. 'We're s'posed to be doing the gravity thing.' I try and grab the mouse off him. But Knaggs pushes me off with his left arm and holds the mouse away from me with his right.

'Get off me, you gay!' he says.

Mr Hambleton comes over. 'What's all the fuss about, boys?' he says.

Knaggs looks up at him. 'David's trying to stop me using the mouse, sir,' he says. 'And it's my turn.'

'He's not doing it properly. He's searching for the wrong things!' I say.

Mr H ignores us both. He's staring at the screen. At the first slide, with the picture of the murderer on it. 'Who's that?' he says.

Quick as a flash, Knaggs says, 'It's an astronaut, sir. Some Russian bloke.'

Mr H nods his head, like he's agreeing with what Knaggs says. 'OK, you mean a cosmonaut, Paul. Well, get on sensibly, boys,' he says. And he's off around the classroom again.

Straight away Knaggs looks around the ICT room. 'Oi, Wood,' he calls.

Wood is at a computer on the other side of the room. He looks round.

'Have a look at this, Gary,' Knaggs says. He moves out of the way so that Wood can see it.

Wood looks at our screen. He doesn't know what he's looking at, but he knows it's a wind-up.

'Put "tramp murderer" into Google and that's what you get,' Knaggs says. 'Must be like looking in a mirror, mustn't it, Wood?'

Wood turns round right away.

Knaggs looks at me and laughs. And then he sits there and adds stuff to the slide. First a background. Then some text: 'Gary Wood murders tramps!'

And I sit there and let him do it. Cos I'm a coward. Cos even though I want to stop him, even though I want to tell Mr H, I can't. I'm too scared.

When Knaggs has finished with the text, he starts animating it all, making it appear on the screen in different ways, with sound effects. He turns round again.

'Hey, Wood,' he says. 'Look at it now.'

Wood turns. Knaggs hits 'start slideshow' on the computer. And then the picture of the murderer and the words 'Gary Wood murders tramps!' start dancing all over the screen to gunshot sound effects. Wood sits there and stares at it. And as he stares, his eyes bulge. His jaw clenches. People at other computers look over as well. They look at the computer and they look at Wood, as though they're comparing the picture with Gary's face. And just as I think Wood's about to explode, to come over and grab Knaggs and smash his head into the computer screen, he just turns round and stares at his own computer.

Zoë

After lunch, Mum comes up the stairs. She knocks, peeps round the door and smiles at me like I'm her poorly little girl. 'How are you feeling now?' she says. 'Have you slept?'

'I'm all right, Mum,' I say quietly.

'Have you slept, Zoë?' she says again.

I shake my head.

Mum sighs. 'Listen, Zoë, I've got to go to town and get a few bits and bobs. Do you want to come with me?'

I shake my head.

'Are you sure?' Mum says. 'A trip out might help take your mind off things.'

I smile at her. 'Honestly, Mum, I'm fine,' I say. 'I'll stay here. Maybe I'll have a sleep.'

'OK.' But Mum doesn't really sound like she wants to leave me alone in the house. 'Is there anything I can get you?'

I shake my head.

As soon as Mum's out of the drive, I start getting dressed. I feel manky in this dressing gown. It's making me feel like I'm ill, when I'm not. As soon as I'm dressed, I grab the keys. I'm gonna do it. I've decided. I'm gonna take them back while Mum's out. I have to. Then I can forget about all this crap. Maybe things will get back to normal then. Whatever normal is.

I feel guilty as soon as I'm outside, shifty, like I shouldn't be doing this. I don't want anyone to see me. I don't want people looking at me, wondering why I'm walking around the streets instead of being at school. But most of all, I don't want anyone to see me going back to the house, like I've got something to hide. The police might be there – I know that. I've already worked out what I'll do if they are. I'm gonna look over at the farmhouse from the gate in the field. I'll be able to see if there are any police cars there. And if there are, I'll just go home. I don't know what I'll do with the keys, though. I guess I could throw them somewhere: the middle of a field or something, in the river maybe. But if I do that, I'll always be thinking about them. Thinking about someone finding them. Thinking about my fingerprints all over the keys. I'd look guilty if I threw them away, like I really did have something to hide. And I don't.

I turn right at the end of my road. There's no traffic, as usual. So I walk in the road. Keep going, out of the village. Fields and hedges and a road and nothing else. No cars, no people. Nothing.

My heart's beating fast. I don't feel good. My head's all murky and confused from no sleep. My hands feel sweaty. I feel like I'm getting a headache. But I keep going. I have to do this.

I walk right down the middle of the road, until I reach the farm gate. I climb up on the bottom rung and look over at the farmhouse. It looks empty, like there's no one there. No police cars anyway. But there's tape around the front door of the house. Police tape, blue and white. Does that mean there's police inside? Does it mean it's a crime scene? I thought the police said he'd just drunk himself to death. My heart's really thumping now. I can feel it in my temples and in my throat. And I feel sick again. I don't think I should go in there. I shouldn't risk it. What if there's someone in there? What am I gonna say if they see me sneaking in? *'Oh, sorry, I'm just returning some keys.'*

I can't do it. I've gotta work out what to do with the keys. I turn and rush back home.

David

Knaggs spots Wood out in the playground. Wood's got his head down, like always. Knaggs walks towards him. All I want is for the earth to open up and swallow me. I don't want to see this again. I just want it all to go away.

Knaggs gets close to him before Wood even realises it. 'Hey, Wood,' he says.

Wood looks up. He turns away as soon as he sees him.

'Hey, maybe you should own up to the cops, Wood. Get Zoë off the hook, get her out of prison. Cos you know what happens to girls in prison, don't you?'

Wood turns and looks at Knaggs. Like he can't

decide whether to smack him in the face or not.

'They turn into lesbians with all them other women around!' Knaggs says, laughing. 'I could imagine Zoë turning to the fairer sex, couldn't you?'

And Wood just snaps. He steps straight towards Knaggs and punches him in the stomach. Knaggs kind of folds in two and falls to the ground, almost in slow motion. Wood runs off straight away. He runs across the playground, jumps the churchyard wall and he's gone.

I look at Knaggs sitting there on the playground, grimacing. There's no way I'm helping him up. He deserved that.

'Jesus!' he says. 'Did you see that?'

I ignore him. I look at the wall, where Wood's just gone.

Zoë

When I get back home, I sit there and look at the keys. There are questions buzzing round my head, like, what am I gonna do with them? Where am I gonna hide them? Has anyone noticed that they're not there, in the box on the wall? The more I look at them, the more paranoid I get. And I realise that there's only one person I can talk to, who knows about this, who'll know what to do with the keys. Gary.

I look at the clock. 15:30. If I go now, I might catch him on his way back from the bus stop. If he went to school today, that is.

I go downstairs, leave a note for Mum: *Gone to see Gary*. And then I'm gone.

As I'm walking up to the village green, I see the school bus go along the main road, towards the bus stop. By the time I get near the stop, everyone is off the bus and doing the usual; messing around in the road; crowding around the outside of the shop. I stand there and wait and watch. A few people look at me strangely as they pass. They're probably wondering why I'm standing there, not in school uniform. But there's no sign of Gary. He usually seems to be first off, first away from the bus stop. He must have gone already.

Paul Knaggs is there, though. He spots me and laughs. He starts walking towards me. I should just walk away from him. But I don't. I want to find out if Gary was at school today.

'Hello, Zoë,' he says as he gets near. 'Someone told me you were in prison. Did you escape?'

'You what?' I say.

'The whole tramp thing. You know, you and Gary murdering the tramp? Someone told me they put you in prison.'

'Grow up!'

Knaggs laughs. 'So who did it? You or Wood?'

'Oh, shut up,' I say. 'Look, was Gary at school today?'

Knaggs smiles. 'Didn't you hear?'

'Didn't I hear what?'

'About lover boy. He ran away.'

'What? What do you mean, ran away?'

'He ran away from school!'

I look back at him. Shocked.

'You didn't know? Oh, Zoë, there's so much to tell!' Knaggs says. 'He went a bit crazy today! See, first of all he punched me in the stomach. For no reason, of course. Completely unprovoked. And then when he realised he was in trouble, he just ran away from school, jumped the wall. He's probably on a killing spree by now. I thought he would've come and found you first, though, so you could be like Bonnie and Clyde.'

I don't want to believe what I'm hearing. 'Are you being serious?' I say.

Knaggs nods his head. 'Deadly!' he says in a voice like a vampire. Then he laughs. 'But I wouldn't go looking for him if I was you, Zoë, unless you want to find another body.'

'What?'

Knaggs smiles. 'He looked suicidal, if you ask me,' he says. 'I reckon he's done himself in! About time too, if you ask me.'

I turn away from Knaggs and walk off. He shouts something after me, but I can't hear what it is. My head's too full of information. I don't know what to believe. I probably shouldn't believe any of it. Knaggs is a bullshitter. But the thing is, most of what he said could be true. I can imagine Gary hitting Knaggs and running away from school. I can even imagine him being suicidal. I think. Crap! I have to find him.

My phone. I put his number on my mobile the other night. I'll phone, see if he went to school today, see if he's gone home. I take it out of my pocket and unlock the keys. Search through my contacts. And I ring the number.

It rings. And rings. And rings. My heart's thumping. I think about hanging up, but then someone picks up.

'Hello,' says a voice in a thick Norfolk accent. Not Gary's.

'Is that Gary's dad?'

He says nothing for a few seconds, he just breathes into the mouthpiece. 'Yeah. Why? Who's this?'

'Zoë.'

Silence. Just more breathing.

'I'm Gary's friend, from school.'

Silence again.

'Did Gary go to school today?'

Breathing. 'Of course he did.'

'Is he home now?'

More breathing. 'No, he's bloody not. Why?'

My heart starts to thump again. 'I'm just looking for him, that's all.'

'Yeah?' his dad says. 'Well, so am I. And if you find

him before me, you can tell him he's in big trouble. I'll give that boy a bloody good hiding when I see him!'

And the phone goes dead.

I stare at my phone. Maybe I should have told his dad about what Knaggs said. Maybe I should call the police. Or maybe I'm just overreacting. God! I can't think straight.

I take some deep breaths. Try and think straight. Where would he go? What would he do?

There's only one answer. The farmyard.

PART TWO

Gary

I can remember it really clearly. Dad must have gone to check on Henry. Dad didn't say nothing at first. I came into the kitchen and he was stood by the sink with his back to me. Saturday afternoon, it was. By then, me and Dad didn't really get on. I sat down, didn't say nothing to him. And he didn't say nothing to me. Didn't turn round, either. I got my books out to do my homework. Only, after a few minutes, I realised that something weren't right. There weren't no noise, but I could see Dad's shoulders kind of going up and down a bit.

I didn't really know what to do. I'd seen Dad cry once before in my life, a couple of years earlier. That was when he used to work for Henry. See, a few years ago, one of the cows on Henry's farm got foot-and-mouth disease. Henry's farm was on the news and everything. They closed all the roads off, put tape up, had over the men in boiler suits and all that. It was a complete fucking disaster. And that was the only other time I seen Dad cry: the day they slaughtered the cows. They all went. Got lifted up into a big trailer and got burnt. All them cows that Dad had looked after all his life. A lot of them he'd even helped when they was born. All gone, just like that. He didn't say nothing about it. He just cried once and that was it.

The time he found Henry, neither of us said anything for ages, till I couldn't bear it no more and I said, 'You all right, Dad?'

He didn't answer right away. He brought his hands up to his face and rubbed his eyes. And he turned round. He weren't crying any more. He sighed. 'Old Henry's dead,' he said. He said it really quiet. My dad don't say much quiet. If he says anything, he usually bloody shouts it.

I didn't say anything. I couldn't believe it. No one I knew had died before. Loads of animals and that had, but that's sort of different.

'Stupid bugger went and shot himself,' Dad said.

I didn't say nothing for a bit. I just looked at Dad, with my mouth open. 'Was it an accident?' I said.

Dad shook his head. 'No, boy,' he said. 'He knew what he was doing. Must have been his best shot, though. That dopey bugger usually couldn't hit a bloody elephant at point-blank range . . .' Dad laughed for a second.

I was shocked. Things were rubbish back then. But I still couldn't believe that someone'd shoot himself. Just like that. One second you're alive, then you pull a trigger and you're dead. 'Why?' I asked.

Dad screwed up his face and shrugged his shoulders. 'What's he got to live for? His farm's gone. Animals have gone. He ain't got no kids, no wife – just a load of greedy nephews and nieces. He's best out of it, boy, believe me.' Dad put his hand on my shoulder for a second, and then he went through to the lounge.

That was all he said about it.

Zoë

I run all the rest of the way to the farm. I have a stitch and I feel sick and tired. But I have to get there as quickly as I can, in case he's there. In case I can stop him doing something stupid. Except, as soon as I've walked across the field and I get close to the barn, I have to stop running. All of a sudden I don't want to be there so quick. So I walk. Slowly. Maybe I don't want to see this. Maybe I don't want to know what might be here. I don't want to find another body.

I tiptoe up to the barn and then peer round the corner. And there he is. Gary. Slumped against the side of the tractor, not moving.

'Gary!' I shout and I run across to him.

He looks up, confused. 'What?'

I feel like flinging my arms round him. I'm so relieved. But he doesn't look as though he'd appreciate that. He looks pissed off. So I just smile. 'Oh my God, I'm so glad you're here,' I say. 'I was worried about you!' I sit down on the ground, next to him.

'Were you? Why?' he says.

'I just saw Knaggs. He said something happened at school today.'

Gary looks down at the ground. He picks up a stone and throws it. It smacks against the wall of the barn and then settles on the floor, in the dirt.

'He said he thought you looked like you were gonna kill yourself. I had to find you. Just to make sure.'

Gary looks up at me. He blushes. He doesn't say anything. He looks hurt. He looks like he could cry. 'Is that what you thought I'd do?' he asks. 'Did you think I'd kill myself?'

I look away from him, at the ground. 'No!' I say. 'I didn't. Sorry, I shouldn't have said that. It's just . . . I didn't know what to think. Knaggs made it sound like you were about to slit your wrists or something. I just wanted to make sure you were safe, that's all. I was worried about you. There's nothing wrong with that.'

He takes a deep breath, puts his head in his hands. 'Why does everyone think I'm fucked in the head?' he says. He looks up, across the barn. He shakes his head.

'Maybe they're right. Maybe I am.'

'You're not, Gary,' I say. 'Listen, I didn't think you would. I was worried, that's all. Knaggs made it sound like you'd lost it. I'm sorry, my head's a bit fuzzy today.'

Gary shakes his head. He rubs his face with his hands.

I'm not handling this right. Everything I say makes it sound like I think Gary's some weirdo. And I don't think that. I take a deep breath, start again. 'Knaggs said you hit him. He said you ran away from school. He said you looked really pissed off, like you'd do something stupid. I couldn't tell if he was taking the piss or not.'

Gary shrugs.

'I called your house. Your dad said he hadn't seen you, said that he was looking for you . . .'

Gary looks up. 'You spoke to my dad?'

I nod.

'Why?'

'I was looking for you.'

'What did he say?'

I scratch my head, try and think it through. I don't want to say the wrong thing here. I've said enough wrong things already. 'Nothing else. He just said to tell you that he was looking for you as well. That's all.'

Gary nods his head really slowly. He looks down at the ground.

'Are you all right, Gary? Are you in trouble with your dad or something?'

He doesn't answer. He just screws up his face like he's in pain. And then he sits there, sighing, making his fingers into a fist and then releasing them again.

It's quiet in the barn. I can hear a few birds twittering. The sun's out now. It's shining in through the front of the barn and through a couple of gaps in the roof tiles. I get up, walk around, look around. Gary is still leaning against the tractor wheel. In my pocket I can feel the keys. I'd almost forgotten about them. I take them out and turn them round and round in my hand. I look at the badge on the fob.

'Hey, Gary,' I say. 'Look what I found last night, in my pocket.' I go and crouch in front of him, hold the keys out for him to look at.

Gary stares at them. His eyes kind of light up. 'Where'd you find them?'

'They were on the wall in the farmhouse. I must have picked them up yesterday and forgot to put them back.'

There's a smile on Gary's face. His eyes are fixed on the keys. 'You know what they're for, don't you?'

'Tractor keys,' I say. 'Will you help me put them back in the house? I don't wanna get in trouble for stealing them.'

Gary holds out his hand. 'Give them here a sec.'

I pass the keys over. I'm glad to be rid of them.

He holds them in his hands, holds them up to his face and examines them, like they're a precious diamond and not a tatty old set of keys. He tosses them up into the air and then catches them. 'I've just had an idea,' he says.

'What?'

Gary doesn't answer. He gets up from the ground and climbs up into the tractor. He smiles at me.

I stand up to get a better look at what he's doing.

Gary puts one of the keys into the tractor ignition and turns it. The engine coughs as it tries to start. It splutters and dies.

'Gary? Stop messing around. Let's go and put the keys back before someone notices they've gone.'

He turns the key again. The engine whirrs then splutters again. Then nothing.

'Gary, what are you doing?'

Gary turns the key again. The tractor whines and coughs. 'Start, you bugger, start!' he shouts. The engine splutters and then bursts into life. Gary looks at me and smiles.

'Gary,' I shout. 'Stop messing about! Can we just put the keys back? This place is making me nervous. You're making me nervous . . .'

Gary shakes his head. He's still smiling. But he

looks a bit mad. 'Jump in!' he shouts.

I look around the field. No one's here. No one's watching. I could just get in, drive around the fields with him. But what if someone does see? How are we gonna explain this away? I shake my head.

The smile fades from Gary's face. 'Come on, Zoë,' he says. 'I know how to drive it. No one'll see us. Just round the field.'

I sigh. I look down at the ground. And then I look up at Gary's face again. He smiles.

'Once round the field and then we put the keys back?' I say.

Gary smiles. He nods.

I climb up into the tractor and sit beside him. This is a bad idea, I know it. This is a really stupid thing to do. But next to me, Gary's grinning like a kid in a sweet shop. He puts the tractor in gear, puts his foot on the accelerator, and off we go.

The tractor wobbles out of the barn. Gary looks at me and smiles this manic grin. I don't think I've seen his face look like that before. It would be nice, if it wasn't for the fact that we've stolen a tractor and my safety is in his hands.

He takes us out into the field. His eyes are fixed ahead now, really concentrating. But this doesn't feel right. If someone sees us we're in loads of trouble.

'I don't think we should be doing this, Gary,' I say.

'What if someone sees us?'

Gary doesn't take his eyes off the field in front. 'Relax, Zoë,' he says. 'We aren't gonna go on any roads. It ain't against the law to drive a tractor in a field.'

I snort with laughter. But I don't think this is very funny. 'We stole the bloody tractor, Gary!' I say. '*That's* against the law!'

Gary laughs. 'That ain't stealing, really. That was Henry's tractor and he's dead. Lazy bugger didn't leave a will, so no one owns it now. I think he'da wanted me to drive it!'

'Will you stop the tractor now, please, Gary?' I say.

But Gary ignores me, turns the wheel and steers round an old trailer. I'm starting to panic. What on earth am I gonna do about this? Someone's gonna notice us, they're bound to. And then what'll happen? I'll get a bloody criminal record and Mum and Dad'll never let me out of the house again. Jesus!

'Stop, Gary!' I shout. 'Please stop it! Let's go and put the keys back!'

He doesn't. He stares out of the front of the tractor, puts his foot down, and we go faster. He steers in and out of the rusty tractors and machines, and he drives faster and faster and faster, so fast that I think the tractor's gonna tip over.

'Gary! Please!'

But he isn't listening any more. And the smile's

gone from his face. Now he just looks manic. He keeps racing the tractor, in and out of the rusty machines. And the more I shout, the more manic and determined he becomes. I don't know what to do. I don't know how to stop him.

Gary turns the tractor towards the gate. He looks at me and smiles.

'Don't!' I say. 'I mean it!'

He heads straight for the gate.

'You're gonna hit the gate!' I shout. 'Stop!'

Gary's smile gets wider. He locks his arms tight on the wheel and we drive towards the gate. I lean over, try to grab the wheel off him, try to steer away from the gate. But Gary's much too strong.

We smash through the gate and on to the road.

'You idiot!' I shout at him.

'Sorry,' he says. But he doesn't look sorry. He's smiling again. 'I couldn't resist the gate! I've always wanted to do that!'

I shake my head. What can I say? I can't think of a way to stop this from happening. I try closing my eyes really tightly, wishing that none of this was happening. But when I open them, we're still in the tractor and we're driving away from Wallingham, down a tiny little road.

'You're gonna get us in so much trouble, Gary,' I say.

He doesn't look at me. He's too busy looking at the

road. He shrugs. 'No one cares about Henry's gate, Zoë,' he says. 'And no one's gonna miss his tractor. Relax.'

Relax? Ha! Yeah, right. I cover my face with my hands and scream into them.

Gary slows the tractor at a crossroads. I think about opening the door, jumping out. But Gary quickly turns the tractor to the right, up another country lane. There's nothing about – no houses, no cars, no people. Only fields all around, flat, stretching for miles.

'Gary, please, someone's gonna see. We can't do this. Let's take the tractor back, before anyone notices.'

'No one'll notice us,' he says. 'There are tractors on the road all the time round here. There ain't nothing strange about that.'

'There is something strange about two kids driving a tractor! You're still in school uniform, for God's sake!' I say. 'What if the police see us?'

Gary laughs. 'When was the last time you saw a policeman round here?'

'How about yesterday?' I say. 'Or have you forgotten?'

He stops smiling. 'Yeah, I mean apart from that.'

I don't remember ever seeing the police round here before that. Although it has only been a week. I shrug.

'Exactly,' he says. 'There ain't no bloody police round here!'

There's no point in arguing with Gary. So I sit there instead and shake my head, just so he knows that I think we're doing a stupid thing. But I don't say anything and neither does Gary. He sits upright and turns the steering wheel and I watch him. It should look all wrong, a school kid driving a tractor. But for some reason, Gary just looks right sitting there, holding the wheel. He doesn't look like a school kid. He looks like he was made to drive this bloody tractor. I guess he looks confident sitting there, high above the road, looking out at the fields. If you ignore the bum-fluff moustache on his top lip, you'd say he was just a farmer, driving to his field, or whatever it is that farmers do. And as I watch him drive, some of his confidence must start to rub off on me, cos I don't feel as nervous any more.

Gary takes the tractor down little road after little road. We go past massive fields full of stuff I don't know the names of. Along dark little roads, surrounded by woods, where the trees bend low over the road, like spooks on a ghost train. We don't pass a single house or person or car. And I start to relax a bit more. Not enough to actually want to be here, just enough to not be shouting at Gary.

The way Gary's taking us down all these tiny, windy roads makes me start to think that maybe he knows what he's doing. He probably knows all these roads like the back of his hand. He's probably planned this all out – the tractor, the route, everything. I look at him again. He looks like a king or something, sat there on the dirty brown seat, holding the wheel. He's got a big smile on his face. He looks different when he smiles. Happier, of course. But more than just that.

'Where are we going?' I ask him.

Gary looks away from the road for a second and smiles at me. 'Dunno,' he says. 'Not much further, though, that's for sure.' And he taps a dial behind the steering wheel that shows a fuel pump. The dial's in the red. And a little red light's on next to it.

'Are we running out of petrol?' I say.

He nods. 'Diesel. Yeah.'

'How far will we get?'

He shrugs. 'Dunno,' he says. Then he slams his foot on the brake and steers in, towards the verge. 'Duck down,' he says.

I do what he says. Lie down on the floor of the tractor cab. It's dirty and smelly. There are huge clods of dried mud and old fag ends.

'What is it?' I say.

'Car,' Gary says. 'Stay still and shut up.'

Crap! This is it. This is the moment when my life changes for ever. They're gonna see Gary and see he's just a kid and they're gonna call the police. And I'm gonna have a criminal record for the rest of my life.

But I do what Gary says. I lie there on the dirty floor, and wait. My heart's beating like mad; I can hear it in my ears, even above the sound of the engine. I'm breathing really quick, shallow breaths. But Gary sits there and waves at the car as it squeezes past us. He doesn't even flinch - he sits there and looks like a farmer, even in his school shirt.

'You can get up now,' he says. 'Car's gone.'

I get up off the floor and sit back down. And I look at Gary as he steers the tractor back out on to the road. 'How'd you do that?'

He looks at me, confused. 'What?'

'Just then. They didn't even notice you. How'd you get away with it?'

Gary shrugs. 'Dunno.'

We drive for about five minutes more before Gary says, 'We're running out of diesel. I'm gonna pull over.'

The engine sounds different, kind of chuggy. It doesn't sound good. Gary drives along slowly, until we get to a break in the hedge and a little track. It leads off the road to a gate with a field the other side. Gary pulls in and puts the handbrake on. He jumps down from the tractor, opens the gate and then gets back in again. We drive through the gate and into the field. We both climb out and I feel relieved.

'What shall we do with it?' I say.

Gary shrugs. 'Nothing much we can do with it. Just leave it there.'

'But it's Henry's tractor, you said. You can't just leave it there.'

Gary walks away from the tractor. 'Henry's dead, Zoë,' he says. 'His stupid divvy family won't even notice it's gone.'

How can I argue with that? What am I gonna do, push it all the way back to Henry's farm? So I shrug as well. We walk back along the path to the road. Gary shuts the gate behind us.

'Where are we, Gary?'

Gary looks up and down the road. 'Not sure,' he says. 'We should be somewhere near the coast, I think. Let's go this way.'

He starts walking up the road. I follow. I don't really have any other choice.

The sun's getting lower in the sky across the field where we left the tractor. It's quite warm, quite nice. It would feel quite relaxing, if I were here on holiday with my family. But I'm not. We've just stolen a tractor and dumped it in a field. And I have no idea where we are or how we'll get home. I feel nervous, guilty.

After a few minutes we come to a crossroads. There's an old-fashioned signpost dug into the grass verge: *Ickley*, *Hinglesthorpe*, *Saltgate*, *Roughley*, *East Strand*.

The names mean nothing to me. I've never heard of any of these places before in my life. Gary looks at the sign and then looks up the road, straight ahead.

'We should go this way,' he says.

'Why? Is it the way home?'

Gary shakes his head. 'No, it's the way to East Strand. Look – "One and a quarter miles". My nan used to take me there when I was little. It's a seaside town.'

I nod my head. We cross the road and set off towards East Strand.

'Is she nice, then, your nan?'

Gary looks at me. 'Yeah,' he says quietly.

'She alive?'

Gary shakes his head and looks away.

'What happened?'

Gary sighs. 'Cancer,' he says. 'She used to smoke like a chimney. When I was about twelve she started getting ill. Died in hospital couple of months later.'

I feel bad now. I don't look at Gary. 'I'm sorry.'

He looks at me and gives me a little smile. 'Don't have to say you're sorry,' he says. 'Weren't your fault.' And he turns away again.

We walk. Silence. Gary's thinking about his nan, I can tell. And I'm starting to worry about the time. I take my phone out of my pocket and check the clock. Nearly five. Mum'll start to worry soon.

After a bit the road gets a little wider. There are a few houses by the side of the road now, thinly spaced out to start with, but the further we walk, the closer together they are.

'Is this it? East Strand?'

Gary stops walking and stares ahead. 'Think so,' he says. 'I've never been to this bit before, though.'

A minute or so later and there are no fields, just houses and a wider road and a pavement. There are even street lights, but they're not on yet. I'm starting to feel excited instead of nervous. I love the seaside. But then I feel something in my pocket. My phone. It's vibrating and ringing. I take it out.

'Oh no!'

Gary looks at me. 'What?'

'It's my mum. She's phoning me. What shall I do?'

Gary looks panicked all of a sudden. 'I dunno. Answer it?'

'But she'll want to know where I am.'

'Just lie,' Gary says.

I look at the phone, watch it vibrate, listen to the crap *bring-bring* ringtone I have. I can't make up my mind what to do. Answer it and I'm in trouble. Don't answer it and she'll probably send out a search party.

But the decision's made for me. My phone stops ringing. My heart sinks. I should have answered it. Shit! Mum'll be even more worried now. Maybe I should call her straight back. But there's no need cos my phone starts to vibrate again and then my crap ringtone starts up again too. I answer it.

'Hello, Mum. Sorry – I couldn't get my phone out of my pocket quick enough.'

'That's all right, love. Where are you? Are you OK?'

My heart starts thumping like a drum against my ribs. Normally I'm quite good at lying. Well, little white lies I'm good at. But this feels like *way* more than that. What shall I say? I need to think of something, quick. 'I'm at Gary's still,' I say. 'He's got some homework that he needs help with.'

'Oh. That's nice,' Mum says. 'Tea's going to be ready in about half an hour, Zoë. Will you be back?'

I panic. There's no way I could be back in half an hour. I don't even know if I want to be back home in half an hour. 'I'm gonna eat here,' I say. 'Gary's mum cooked us some pasta.'

Gary looks at me like I've gone mad. But then he smiles.

'OK, love,' Mum says. 'But don't be too late. Just give us a buzz if you want a lift.'

'All right, Mum. Bye. Love you.' I hang up and breathe a sigh of relief. And I switch my phone off.

'Did she believe you?' Gary asks.

'Not sure,' I say. 'Think so.'

We carry on walking, towards the town. The air

smells salty. It reminds me of Granny's house – she lived near the sea. I love the smell of the seaside. There are seagulls wheeling around the sky but I feel weird. What am I doing?

I sit down on the beach and look out to sea, breathe in the salty air. Gary walks straight down to the shore. He picks up stones and tries to skim them across the water. He's not very good at it, though. Mostly the stones sink straight away. Just occasionally he gets one to skip across before it sinks. But I'd say the sea looks too choppy to skim stones properly. When I was about eight, Dad tried to teach me how to skim stones. We were on holiday in Kent, near Granny's house. I tried it, but I couldn't throw them flat enough or fast enough. Dad got really peed off in the end, trying to teach me. He'd have liked a son to do that sort of stuff with, I think. I s'pose he might get a chance to one day, if the baby's a boy, if I have a brother. But by the time the kid's old enough to skim stones, Dad'll virtually be a pensioner. He'll be over fifty. My God! I hadn't thought of that before. That's awful!

Gary walks back up the beach. He looks at the ground, searching for stones, I guess. He picks up a massive one. He doesn't bother trying to skim this one, just lobs it up into the air as high as he can and then watches it plummet and disappear into the sea with a *sploosh*. He turns round and walks up the beach, towards me.

'You all right, Gary?'

He nods, sits down and looks out to sea.

'It's nice here, isn't it?'

Gary nods again.

'Do you come here a lot?'

'Not much any more. But Nan used to love it. She used to bring me here all the time.'

I smile at Gary, but he's too busy looking at the sea to notice.

We sit there for a while, not really doing anything. We both look out to sea. I watch a ship. It must be miles away; it looks tiny. It slowly passes along the horizon. It looks like it's carrying containers. I start to wonder where it came from, try to picture a map of Britain in my head. I think it must have come from the east – maybe from Holland or Germany or somewhere like that. Although I guess it could have come from further away – China maybe, or Korea. I watch until it's behind the pier.

I look across at Gary. He isn't looking out to sea any more. He's curled up, almost in a ball, his head in his hands. I think he might be crying. He's not making any noise, though.

'Are you OK, Gary?'

He doesn't look up. He just kind of nods his head,

rocks backwards and forwards a bit. I put my hand on his back. He tenses up at my touch.

'What's the matter?'

Gary takes his head out of his hands and sits up. He looks at the waves and takes a deep breath. 'Nothing. Just thinking about stuff,' he says.

I'm not sure what to say. I can't tell if he wants me to ask him about it or not. But sitting here in silence doesn't seem like the right thing to do. So I say, 'About what happened at school today?'

Gary shrugs.

I don't know what to do, what to say. I rub his back a little. But it feels wrong, so I take my hand away again.

Slowly, Gary turns to me. 'Everyone thinks I'm mental or something,' he says. He looks straight at me for a few seconds, like he's begging me to do something, to say something, to help him. Then he turns away again.

And I know that I should say something. 'They don't!' I say. 'Who does?'

'Everyone,' he says. He picks up a stone and throws it out to sea.

'Don't be stupid. You're being paranoid,' I say. But I know that's not true. People do think he's weird, a loner, mental. They think *I'm* weird just cos I talk to him.

Gary picks up another stone and hurls it out to sea.

'They do,' he says. 'Everyone at school does – Knaggs and all his mates. All the teachers do. My mum. My dad. They all think I'm wrong in the head.'

'You're not!'

'You weren't there today. Everyone thinks I murdered the medal man!' he says.

'Of course they don't,' I say. 'They're just having a laugh. You have to ignore them, Gary. Anyway, I bet that was just Knaggs, wasn't it?'

Gary nods. He sighs. He looks down at his feet. He starts to move them back and forth in the pebbles, so that they sink down, get covered in stones. 'If no one thinks I'm mad, then how come they want me to go to some sodding shrink?' he says. His voice is angry, cracked. He looks at me. His eyes are red and wet.

I still don't know what to say. I sit and look at him, helpless. I feel like I should put my arms round him or something, give him a hug. He looks like he needs it. But something stops me. 'Just cos you've got to go and see someone, doesn't make you mad, Gary,' I say. 'Loads of people have to see someone – a therapist or whatever.'

He looks away, shakes his head. He wipes his eyes with his hand, looks out again across the sea. He looks really tense.

'My best friend – back in London – she has to go

and see someone. A psychiatrist,' I say. 'And she isn't mad.'

'Good for her,' Gary says. 'But I ain't gonna go and see no one.'

We sit there for a bit, both looking out to sea and thinking. I should be saying something right now. I should be saying something that helps Gary. But I really don't know what that thing is, otherwise I'd say it in a second. So I sigh instead and look at the waves breaking, watch a couple of kids trying to race the waves back up the beach.

'Why does she have to go?' Gary says. He says it really nervously.

I turn and look at him. 'Who?'

'Your friend. Why does she have to go and see a shrink?'

I sigh. I'm not sure if I should talk about this. It's confidential, I guess. Although Jodie never holds back on the details. And besides, if she could see Gary right now, I think she'd understand. 'She used to self-harm,' I say quietly.

Gary looks at me blankly.

'She used to cut herself when she felt bad,' I say. 'Still does sometimes, I think.'

Gary winces. He looks shocked, horrified. 'Jesus!' he says. 'Why does she do that?'

I look down at the ground. I think about Jodie. And

I shrug. 'Dunno really. Neither does she. That's why she goes to see someone, I guess.'

Gary turns away again. I'm not sure if I've made him feel better or worse.

'There's nothing wrong with getting help, Gary,' I say. 'It's people that say they don't need help that are really messed up.'

Gary looks at me. He smiles. Then he turns away again, picks up another stone and lobs it into the water.

'Really, Gary, I mean it. You're not mental, you're not mad. Everyone needs help sometimes.'

Gary pulls his feet up, out of the pebbles. Stones drop down from his big boots, on to the beach. He gets up and brushes himself down. 'Come on,' he says. 'Let's go for a walk.'

There's a sign above the door. *Twiddy's Amusements*, it says in peeling paint.

'You got any money?' Gary says.

I shake my head. 'Not much.'

Gary puts his hands into his pockets. When he pulls them back out, they're filled with coins. Mostly silver. 'Come on, let's go in,' he says.

It's noisy inside. Sirens, bells, buzzers, the *chug-chug-chug* as a machine pays out. Gary stands there and takes it all in. He smiles. Over to the left I can see the machines where you drop in 2p coins – the ones where there are two or three shelves that move and sometimes knock the coins off. I don't know what they're called. '2p machines' probably. But I remember going on one in Folkestone. I won 14p. Probably put more than that into the machine, though.

'Can we go on the 2p machines?' I say to Gary.

Gary looks over. He sort of sneers at the machines. And I feel really small and stupid. '*You* can if you want,' he says. 'I'm going on the fruity.' And he points over to the big bank of buzzing, flashing fruit machines.

'I haven't got enough money for that,' I say. 'Anyway, don't you need to be eighteen or something?'

Gary shrugs. 'So?'

I shrug as well. 'Please yourself.' I head over to the 2p machine.

In my purse I have eight 2ps and a 5p. I stand by the machine, try and find a place to drop my money into where there are loads of coins hanging over the edge of the shelf. I drop a coin in. It slides down the machine and lands in a gap on the top shelf, just as the shelf moves forward. Then the shelf moves back and my coin squashes the others up. But none fall off. 2p wasted.

I watch the machine for a few seconds, try and get into the rhythm of the shelves, moving backwards and forwards. I feel like a high-jumper, rocking backwards and forwards, waiting for the right moment to start my run-up. Then I try again, drop in a coin. It slides down and lands on the top shelf as it moves forward. The shelf comes back and my coin squashes against all the others. One drops off the edge, on to the middle shelf. My heartbeat quickens. I stare at the coin that's fallen. The middle shelf comes back and squeezes my coin against the others. I hold my breath. But nothing falls.

I do it again and again and again. No luck. In two minutes I have lost my complete collection of 2ps. All I have left is my 5p coin. There's a 5p machine next to me. I look at it, watch the shelves move, watch the silver coins squash against each other. I'm tempted. But then I sigh and I put the coin away. Gambling sucks. Especially if you don't win.

I walk over to Gary. He's staring at the fruit machine. His face glows orange and red as the lights on the machine flash. It doesn't look like the first time he's played these machines. His hand seems to naturally rise to the slot as he drops coin after coin in with a *clunk*. He looks like he should be smoking a fag, a pint rested on top of the machine.

'Any luck?'

He shakes his head and he sighs. He doesn't take his eyes off the machine. 'I don't think it's paying out.' He hits a button and the fruits spin round. 'Bollocks!' he says.

'Maybe you should stop,' I say. 'Come on, let's go somewhere else.'

Gary shakes his head. He puts his hand into his pocket and pulls out a £1. 'This is my last coin,' he says. 'You put it in for me.'

I look at him and then at the coin. I should just take it and run out of the arcade, save it so we can get some crisps or a drink or something. But Gary's face pleads with me. I take the coin from him and put it into the machine. *Clunk*. The machine starts to buzz and flash.

'What do I do?' I say.

Gary leans over and points at a flashing button. 'Press that one,' he says.

So I do. The fruits twirl round. Two watermelons and some cherries.

'Hold them two and nudge that one,' he says.

'What?'

He leans over again. 'Press that one and that one. Right, and now press that one.'

I do what he says. Three watermelons. The machine plays a little tune and the lights go mad, flashing.

'Have we won?'

'Sort of,' Gary says. 'Let me do this bit.'

I move out of the way and Gary starts pressing buttons and getting excited. After a minute, the machine starts to *chug-chug-chug* as it pays out. Gary turns to me.

'We done it!' he says. 'Thirty-five quid jackpot!'

'Really?' I say. 'Woohoo!'

Gary scoops the money out of the machine. He gives me a big handful of coins and puts the rest in his pocket. Then he takes a £1 coin and goes to put it back in the machine.

'What are you doing, Gary?'

He stops, looks at me. 'What? I'm gonna try and win some more.'

I shake my head. 'Don't be stupid,' I say. 'Come on, let's go. The noise in here's doing my head in.'

Gary looks like he wants to stay, though. Probably till they shut the place up tonight, if he can. He'll just put the whole lot back in if he's allowed, I know it.

'Please,' I say, 'can we go somewhere else?'

Gary's about to say something, when a little bald bloke in a white shirt and red tie comes marching over towards the machines. He looks at me with my handful of coins. And he looks at Gary, stood at the machine in his school uniform – white shirt and black trousers. It's obvious what he's thinking. He stops between us.

'How old are you, young lady?' he says.

I can feel myself blushing. I panic. My heart starts beating like mad. What do I say? He's never gonna believe I'm eighteen. 'Seventeen,' I say. 'Nearly eighteen.'

'Really?' he says. He smiles at me patronisingly. 'So what year were you born?'

I look at him. My mind's gone completely blank. I can't work it out quick enough. I look at Gary, but he just shrugs and looks away. So I try and take a deep breath and work it out . . . But it's too late. I took too long. He knows I'm working it out in my head.

'Go on, on your bike,' he says.

I put the coins in my purse and head away from the machines. Gary stands there, staring.

'And you, sonny,' the little bald bloke says, 'vamoose, scram, beat it.'

Gary stares at him, stares him right in the face. Gary's actually taller than the bald bloke. The bald bloke smiles at him, a really smug little smile. Gary barges past.

We step outside, out of the noise of the arcade and on to the street. It feels cooler than before. There are seagulls circling around, calling. And I can smell chips.

'You hungry?'

Gary nods his head.

'Wanna go get some chips?'

Gary smiles. 'Definitely,' he says. 'I know this place that does really good fish and chips. Follow me.'

* * *

It's the kind of chip shop where you can sit down at a table to eat. Toni's Plaice, it's called. I love cheesy names like that. We choose a table near the window and sit down. Gary sits opposite me. He smiles at me, but then he looks away again almost straight away. He picks up a menu from the table. I do the same. The first thing I do is look at the prices, see what I can afford. It's what Mum and Dad always do if we go out. I get told what I'm allowed to have and what I'm not. But with more than ten quid in my purse, I can have what I like for a change. So I think I'll have a burger and chips and a can of Coke.

'What are you gonna have, Gary?'

Gary closes his menu with a snap and puts it down on the table. 'Easy,' he says. He smiles. 'Skate and chips, mushy peas and Shandy Bass!'

I screw my face up. 'Ugh! How could you?'

Gary looks at me. He does something with his face that makes him look like a hurt puppy. 'What?' he says. 'What's wrong with that?'

I smile. 'Mushy peas! And fish!'

He looks like he doesn't understand me. 'It's good for you,' he says. 'Fish makes you brainy!'

'Tastes grim, though.'

'It's what my nan used to have,' Gary says, looking away from me again. He looks around the chip shop and takes it all in.

There's a silence. I start to think about Mum and Dad at home, wondering when I'm coming back. They'll probably be trying to get through to me on my mobile. Mum will at any rate. Dad'll probably be off in a world of his own, rearranging his socks in alphabetical order or something. But Mum'll be sitting on the sofa, her face creased and wrinkled, thinking about all the trouble that I might have found. Maybe I should switch my phone on, just in case she calls. I could make up another excuse, try and buy Gary and me some time to get back home. It looks like we're gonna need it. I take my phone out of my pocket.

Gary looks up straight away. He looks at my phone. 'What are you doing?'

'Nothing.' The way Gary's looking at me makes me feel guilty. 'I just wanted to know what time it is.'

Gary points behind me. There's a clock up on the wall, a novelty one. No numbers on it, just fish. It says half past haddock. Half six. I sigh. Mum'll definitely be worried by now. She'll be looking Gary's family up in the phone book. Or at least she would be if she knew his last name. Either way, I'll be in trouble. I put my phone away again.

Gary looks around the shop. 'It hasn't changed much,' he says.

It doesn't look like anything's been changed in here for about fifty years. There are a couple of faded posters saying how healthy fish and chips are; another has different species of fish on it. There's a carved wooden fish on the counter and next to that there are two sailor hats. It's cheesy but it all looks clean.

'Did your nan bring you here, then?'

Gary nods. 'Always,' he says. He smiles. 'She reckoned they did the best chips in the whole of Norfolk.'

I smile. 'And do they?'

'Yes we do, madame,' says a voice over to my right. It's a waiter; he has a pad of paper in his hand. 'What would you like?'

We order and the waiter goes off behind the counter. And when he's gone, we sit there in silence. I smile at Gary. He kind of half smiles back and then looks away. So we sit there in silence again. Gary looks around the place, at the posters and stuff. He plays with the sauce bottles. And I sit there and think about Mum thinking about me. Getting in the tractor was not a good idea. It's been fun, don't get me wrong, but I just know there's gonna be trouble later. I have to go back soon, before Mum starts calling the police and sending out search parties and stuff. Before she starts to think that I've run away from home. I mean, it might not be the greatest place to be – home – but there's no way I'd run away. I have no idea how we'll get back, though. Are there buses from here to Wallingham? And I still don't even know if Gary is coming home. Maybe this is it for him from now on: stealing tractors, playing fruit machines, eating chips . . .

My thoughts are interrupted. The waiter's back at our table. He puts our plates and our drinks in front of us.

'Enjoy your meal.' And he's gone again.

'This looks good!' I say. I take my knife and fork out of the napkin.

Gary nods. He's already shovelling food into his mouth.

We sit and eat in silence. I say eat, but I just sit there and pick at my burger and chips. I don't feel that hungry any more. I feel like I should be at home. And besides, Gary's nan was wrong – these chips suck. Still, Gary scoffs like he hasn't eaten for a year. And he drains his Shandy Bass in about two gulps. When he finishes, I push my half-full plate into the middle of the table.

'Help yourself. I'm not all that hungry.'

Gary looks at the plate and then at me, trying to decide whether it's polite to eat my plateful as well. He should know better than to try to be polite around me. He grabs a chip off the plate and shoves it in his mouth.

'That was nice,' I say.

He smiles. 'Told you! Best chips in Norfolk.'

He helps himself to more of my chips. I check the

clock again. It's nearly plaice o'clock. Seven. Mum'll probably be on the phone to the police by now. I feel homesick. It seems stupid. But I just want to be home. Even if 'home' means Wallingham and not Morden. I want Mum and Dad to know that I haven't run away. Maybe I should switch my phone on and send a text, let them know I'm OK, then switch it off again quick, so they can't call me. I sigh. I look at Gary.

'Have you run away from home?' I ask him. 'Is that what this is all about?'

Gary looks at me. He starts to blush and then looks at the table instead. He makes a face, like he doesn't know what he's doing. He shrugs.

'Are you gonna go back?'

He shrugs again. His eyes start to bulge as he fiddles with the ketchup bottle on the table. He stops, looks up at me. 'Are you? Are you going home?'

I nod. 'Yeah. Of course I am. I have to.'

He looks back at the table. 'I don't want to,' he says. 'I've got no reason to go back. No one even likes me.'

I look at him. Try and catch his eye. But he looks anywhere except in my direction. 'You're being paranoid,' I say. 'Plenty of people like you. Your mum, your dad, me . . .' I want to add to the list, but I've never seen anyone talking to Gary. I don't know who actually likes him. Apart from me. 'Loads of people,' I say.

'My dad don't want me at home,' Gary says. He clenches his jaw.

'Don't be daft,' I say. 'Course he does.'

Gary fidgets. He looks uncomfortable, scared almost. 'No, Zoë, I mean it. Me and my dad, we don't get on.'

I think back to earlier, to when I called his dad. It seems like a lifetime ago. His dad sounded angry. Maybe he hits Gary or something. That might explain a lot.

Gary sighs.

'Why don't you get on?' I say.

'I don't wanna talk about this,' he says, and he gets up. 'I'm gonna pay.'

David

I have more homework. I hate it. It sucks. I'm lying on the floor in my room with all the books I need spread out in front of me. But I haven't done a thing yet. I'm listening to the radio instead, staring at the walls and trying not to think about things too much.

There's a gentle knock on my door. Must be Mum or Dad, cos if it was Ollie, he'd have just barged straight in.

'Come in.'

Mum comes in through the door. She sits down on my swivel chair. It takes ages for her to say anything. But eventually she opens her mouth and says, 'Did something happen again at school today?'

I look blankly back at her. I immediately feel guilty. It's one of those questions that parents and teachers ask when they think you might have done something and want you to drop yourself in it. So I shrug my shoulders. 'What do you mean?'

'I've just had Margaret on the phone,' she says. 'She's in floods of tears.'

'Oh,' I say. I look down at my books on the floor.

'*Did* something happen today?' Mum says.

I don't say anything. I don't even look at her.

Mum sighs. 'Gary hasn't come home,' she says.

I look up at her. She looks serious. She looks as though she's gonna cry. 'What?' I say.

'Margaret hasn't seen him,' she says. 'She doesn't know what's happened to him. She's not sure whether to phone the police or not.'

I stare at Mum. I don't know what to say. I really can't believe what she's just said.

'David, she's beside herself, she's crying and . . .' Mum doesn't finish her sentence. I can see she's got a tear in her eye.

'He'll come back,' I say. 'It's only seven or something, isn't it? He's probably just out with . . .' I was going to say 'friends'.

Mum takes a deep breath. She shakes her head.

I look down at my homework. By the time I look up again, Mum's left the room. And I feel like shit.

Zoë

We walk down the high street. All the lights and stuff are starting to blink on now that the sun's going down. It's started to cloud over as well. There are loads of little tourist shops with postcards and buckets and spades outside them. I love those kinds of shops, I love all the tat they sell. I stop outside one of them and have a look at the display in the window.

'Can I just go in here, Gary?' I say.

Gary shrugs his shoulders. 'If you want.'

So I step inside. Gary doesn't follow me in. The shop's packed full of ashtrays and place mats and fridge magnets, all with *North Norfolk Coast* or *East Strand* written on them. And there's a load of T-shirts on a rail, with tacky slogans like *surf dude*. Over by the counter there are boxes of stuff, like rubbers and pencils and lighters. And right next to the till there's a box filled with bottles of bubble mixture. I pick one up.

'How much is this?'

'Huh?' says the man behind the counter. 'Oh, fifty pence.'

I smile. 'Bargain!' I take a £1 coin out of my purse and hand it to him.

'What's that?' Gary says, when I come back out of the shop.

'Bubbles!' I say. I take the lid off, dip the blower in and then blow some bubbles. They float straight up into the air above our heads.

Gary rolls his eyes and we keep walking. I put the lid back on the bubbles and put it in the front pocket of my hoodie.

It's quite cold outside now. And Gary's just in his short-sleeved shirt. He has goosebumps on his arms.

'Are you warm enough?' I ask him. I sound like my mum.

Gary nods his head. 'I'm all right,' he says. 'Come on, let's go to the pier.'

I shiver and kind of hunch up in my hoodie to keep warm. 'Wait a minute, Gary,' I say. 'I want to check my phone. Mum's probably going crazy by now.'

Gary stops walking. He turns and looks at me. He looks like he wants to say something. But he doesn't.

'You should call your mum too, Gary,' I say. 'She'll be worried about you.'

Gary shifts from foot to foot. 'It'll do her some good to worry about me for a change.'

I take my phone out and switch it on. As soon as it starts up, it vibrates and the message tone beeps: four voice messages and two texts from 'Mum Mobile'. **Are you coming home soon, Zoë? Love, Mum x Love you!** and **Where are you? Shall we come and get you? Give us a call. Mum x**

I want to cry.

'Who's it from?' Gary says.

'My mum,' I say. 'I'm gonna call her. What shall I say?'

Gary shrugs. He puts his hands in his pockets.

'I think I'm gonna ask her to come and get me,' I say. Gary spins on his heels and looks in the other direction. I don't think he wants me to go home. 'She could give you a lift as well if you want, Gary.'

He doesn't turn back to me.

'Gary?' I say.

He just looks at the pier, at the lights winking.

Fuck him, then. I lift my phone to my face. My heart starts to thump. How am I gonna explain this to Mum? I can't just say, *'Can you pick me up from the seaside.'* So I try and think of an excuse. Gary's geography homework was about seaside towns? Gary's mum dropped us off here? But they just sound crap. So I close my eyes and press the green button anyway. It hardly even rings before someone picks it up.

'Hello, Zoë?' Mum says. She sounds worried.

I take a deep breath. I want to cry again. 'Hello, Mum.'

'Oh, thank goodness it's you,' she says. 'I was beginning to think you'd disappeared off the face of the earth! I wish you'd keep your mobile switched on.' She sounds a bit cross, as well as relieved.

'Can you pick me up, please, Mum?'

'Of course, love,' she says. 'Where does Gary live?'

I take a deep breath, look at Gary, at the bright lights on the seafront. 'Um, I'm not at Gary's house,' I say.

There's a silence at the other end of the phone. I can picture Mum's face. I feel guilty just thinking about it. 'Well, where on earth are you, then?' she says.

Now it's my turn to be silent. I look at Gary. He's still looking at the pier. 'I'm at the seaside,' I say quietly.

'You're where?' Mum says. 'Zoë, what's going on? Is Gary there as well? Are you OK?'

'Yeah, I'm fine,' I say. 'We came to see Gary's nan.'

Gary swings round and looks at me. He looks confused.

'She lives in East Strand, Mum. Can you pick us up?'

There's another silence on the other end of the phone. In the background I think I can hear Mum telling Dad where I am. Dad comes on the phone.

'OK, Zoë,' he says. 'What's her address?'

Jesus! What on earth do I say now? Make up an address? Crap. Crap. Crap. Deep breath. 'Oh, we're not at her house any more. We're at the pier now,' I say. 'Gary's nan had to go to bed. And I wanted to see the sea.'

Gary looks at me and shakes his head. But he looks like he's about to smile, like he thinks it's funny.

'What?' Dad says. He sounds cross. 'Just wait there. We'll be there as soon as we can.'

It's silent for a second. I can imagine Dad standing there, frowning. Mum'll be next to him, looking worried. 'Sorry, Dad,' I say.

'Just stay where you are and we'll come and get you. Make sure you don't talk to any strange people. Mum'll phone your mobile when we get near.'

'Love you, Dad,' I say. And I hang up.

Gary looks at me. He looks sheepish, like he feels guilty. 'Were they all right, your mum and dad?'

'Not sure,' I say. 'Don't think they believe me. Still, what can they do?'

Gary looks scared.

'Are you gonna come back with us? There'll be room in the car. They won't mind giving you a lift.'

Gary doesn't nod or shake his head or anything. He just turns, looks at the pier and says, 'So are we gonna go to the pier, then, or what?'

I smile, nod my head. Gary starts walking. I catch up with him and put my arm through his.

We walk to the pier in silence. Arm in arm. It doesn't exactly feel right. But then it doesn't exactly feel wrong, either. Just a bit awkward. The air is damp and salty and cold. There are quite a few other people out for a walk. Mainly old people, but there are some kids hanging about as well. Boys with shaved heads and baseball caps, and girls with hoop earrings. It's like being back in Morden. There are a few people fishing too.

There's a building at the end of the pier. *The New Theatre*, the sign says. It's lit up by hundreds of bright white bulbs. Posters up around the doorway say the Chuckle Brothers are appearing in the holidays. And *Greased Lightning* is on as well, which just looks like a rip-off of *Grease*. We stop in front of it and look.

'Nan used to take me there sometimes,' Gary says suddenly, pointing at the theatre. 'She used to like the "end of the pier show".'

'The what?'

'End of the pier show.'

'What's that?'

Gary shrugs. 'Dunno. Just a show really. They tell jokes and sing and dance and that.'

'Oh,' I say. I don't really know what else to say. 'Is it good?'

Gary looks up at the sky. He's thinking. He smiles. 'Nah. It's shit.'

I laugh.

We start walking again. Round the corner, round the outside of the theatre. It seems to get windier with every step we take. The sea looks quite rough. It's freezing out here.

'Aren't you cold, Gary?'

Gary looks at me and smiles. 'Bit.'

'You can borrow my hoodie if you want. I've got a long-sleeved T-shirt on underneath.'

Gary smiles again. 'Nah. You keep it. It'll be too small for me.'

We stop walking at the end of the pier. I take my arm out of Gary's and we lean on the railings and look out to sea.

'I love the sea. It's really relaxing, isn't it? Just the sound of it,' I say.

Gary nods his head without looking at me. He looks relaxed, almost. More normal anyway.

We stand in silence for a while. In my head I start to think of the excuses I'm gonna give Mum and Dad later on. I'll have to keep the one about visiting Gary's nan going. It might not be all that good an excuse, but Mum and Dad won't know any better unless Gary tells them. And I can't imagine that happening. For a start, I still have no idea whether he's coming home with us or not. I hope he is. I hate to think about what he'll do otherwise. I guess he'd have to sleep rough or something. I don't want him to end up like the medal man – on his own, nothing to live for. But it's Gary's choice. It's probably none of my business. I've only known him for a week. Seems like longer. But I'm not gonna force him to come back – not if he doesn't want to. If things are that bad at home with his dad, maybe he's better off on the streets. And I can understand why he wouldn't want to come back to school with Knaggs there, ready to rip him apart again.

So I make a deal with myself. If Gary decides not to come back, I'll just do what I can. Lend him my hoodie to keep himself warm, cos he'd freeze to death in that shirt. And maybe I'll skive off school sometimes, come here to see him. Maybe even get him to talk to social services. God! How ridiculous is this? I've just decided the rest of his life for him. I've got to stop being so pessimistic.

I look at the time on my mobile. 19:45. I wonder how long it'll take Mum and Dad to get here. They'll be here soon, surely. I hope so. I've had enough of this now. I just want to be back at home. I want things to be normal.

I look over at Gary. He really does look frozen, stood at the end of the pier. His goosebumps are like thousands of little hills on his arms. The sun's right down now.

'Do you wanna go somewhere a bit warmer?' I say.

Gary shakes his head. 'I like it here.'

'But it's freezing. You're getting goosebumps on your goosebumps.'

Gary shakes his head again. But he shivers. I have to do something to warm him up a bit. I move closer to him, so our sides are touching. And then I reach up and put my arm around his shoulders, like a friend. Gary looks at me. He looks a bit shocked. I smile back at him and then look out to sea. Gary just stands there, tense, as though he can't relax with my arm around his shoulders. But after a while he starts to relax.

We stand there for a bit, just quietly looking at the sea and the boats and the moon behind the clouds. Except I'm not *just* looking, I'm thinking as well. About him, about me, about the tractor and the medal man and . . . Just about everything. It's all a blur in my head, one thing blending into all the others. It's a mess. I don't want to think about it. So I talk instead.

'Have you decided if you're going home or not?' I say.

Gary's shoulders stiffen a little. He shrugs.

'You should, Gary,' I say.

He doesn't answer.

'You'll freeze to death if you stay here. And where would you sleep?'

Gary shrugs. 'Don't matter.'

I sigh. I take my arm off Gary's shoulders and look at him. 'You should go and see your mum and dad. I bet they've missed you.'

Gary kind of snorts, but he isn't laughing.

'I'd miss you if you didn't come back to Wallingham,' I say.

Gary looks at the ground shyly. 'Would you?' he says.

I laugh. 'Course I would, stupid.'

I listen to the waves crashing on the beach. I close my eyes, take a deep breath and just listen.

After a few seconds I open them again. And I look at Gary. He's already looking at me. Straight at me. Into my eyes. He never does that. I smile at him. He looks away.

'I like you,' he says quietly. Then he kind of looks shocked, like he can't believe he just said that. He blushes and looks out to the ships sitting on the horizon.

And I know I have to say something. Otherwise it's gonna be awkward. 'I like you as well,' I say. 'You're a good friend, Gary.'

Gary looks at me for a second and smiles. He looks right into my eyes. And it feels really weird. He doesn't look away. He never does this – looks at me for more than a second. And then he closes his eyes, leans forward and moves his head towards me. He's going to kiss me. Oh, Jesus! I move back.

'What are you doing?' I say. And as I say it, I can hear that it doesn't come out right. I sound like I think he's just done the most awful, wrong thing in the world.

Gary opens his eyes and looks at me. He blushes. He looks hurt. 'I –' he says. 'I thought . . .' He doesn't finish his sentence. He looks away, goes red. He marches off, back up the pier.

Shit! 'Gary, come back,' I shout.

He doesn't even turn round.

I watch him as he marches away. It's like I'm paralysed, or in shock. It's only when he disappears round the other side of the theatre that I realise I should do something. So I run after him. He's halfway along the pier by the time I catch him. He doesn't look at me. I try and walk alongside him, try and keep up. I have to jog every few steps.

'Gary, please don't do this!'

He keeps his eyes fixed straight ahead. Not a sign that he's heard me.

'I didn't mean it to sound like it did,' I say.

He doesn't say a word.

'You just took me by surprise, that's all,' I say. 'I'm sorry. Please don't do this.'

He still doesn't look at me. He's not going to. We're near the end of the pier now. I need to do something to stop him. I run a few steps in front and then turn, stand in Gary's way, my hands up.

'Please, Gary, stop,' I plead.

But he doesn't – he just looks away from me and then marches around me instead. He walks along the seafront.

'Gary, my parents are gonna be here soon! Come on, just get a lift home with us. It'll all seem better in the morning, honestly.'

He still doesn't look at me. His head's down now, looking at the ground. And he just stomps along.

I don't know what to do. This is my fault. Cos of the way I reacted. And now I can't stop it. I can't make him see sense. If he wasn't running away from home before, he sure as hell is now. Fuck it! So I do the only thing I can think of. I shout. I scream, 'STOP BEING SUCH A DICK, GARY! TALK TO ME!'

Gary stops. He looks at me. I can't tell if he's angry or annoyed or confused or what. I don't think he can, either. There are other people now, staring at us.

I lower my voice. 'Gary, please, I didn't mean to hurt your feelings. Please come back with me. You just took me by surprise.'

Gary looks at me. He doesn't say anything for a few seconds. Then he opens his mouth. 'I'm not coming back,' he says quietly. 'Just leave me alone. Go back to your mum and dad.'

And he walks off again. He doesn't march this time. And I don't think I'm gonna stop him. I don't think I'm gonna change his mind. I watch him go, for a bit. He walks past the arcades and the pubs and the chip shops without looking back. And then I think of him spending the night outside, in just that shirt. I take my hoodie off and chase after him.

'Gary, take this,' I say. 'You'll freeze to death otherwise.'

He takes the hoodie off me, but he doesn't put it on. He says 'thank you' really quietly and walks off again. And I let him go.

Gary

I walk. I don't know what else I can do. I don't want to be there any more. I don't want to see East Strand pier again for the rest of my life. I hope the stupid fucking thing burns down. D'you know what? Maybe I should do it myself. Get some matches, get some petrol. Boom! The end. If I'm lucky, I might kill myself while I'm doing it.

I've got no idea where I'm going. I just keep walking, don't look back. Don't take long to get out of the high street – a couple of minutes maybe. Then I'm out into some roads where there's a load of houses and pavements and street lights. A couple of minutes more and there are no more houses and there ain't a pavement, either, just a grass verge. I walk along it, off the road. There's normally a load of dickheads driving their souped-up cars round these roads like they're driving round bloody Silverstone. Boy racers. So there ain't no way I'm walking on the road. I don't want to die. Not like that.

The moon's out. It's bloody cold now. It's always colder at the coast. It's the winds coming in off the North Sea. Nan used to say that they come all the way from the North Pole.

Zoë's given me her jumper. I've got it in my hands. I didn't want to put it on when she could see me. I wanted her to think I didn't need it. But I'm gonna put it on. I'm shivering. There ain't no way I'm going back to Wallingham, and if I'm gonna stay out here, I gotta keep warm. I stop by the side of the road and pull it over my head. It's quite tight round the shoulders, but it'll keep me warm. It smells clean. Girly. Like Zoë. And as soon as I smell it, I can feel my cheeks going red. I'm blushing. I can't believe what a dick I've been. Jesus Christ! What was I thinking? I can't believe I've just done that. How could I think that she'd fancy me? What an idiot. I've gone and messed it up. I messed everything up. We can't even be friends now, not after that.

I don't even know whether we was proper friends anyway. She just felt sorry for me. Poor little mental

Farmer Boy. And the truth is, she don't even know who I am, not really. She don't even care, as long as she makes herself feel good. And d'you know what? I don't need it. I don't need no one to feel sorry for me. I wish everyone'd just leave me alone instead of interfering. Just leave me alone.

David

My phone beeps. It's on the floor, next to the homework I should be doing. I get off my bed and reach it. It's a text from Knaggs: **Wood stole a tractor! He's run away from home with Z!**

I stare at my phone. I have to read the message again. And again. And again. And I still can't believe it. I sit down on my bed and send him a text back: **What u mean? U serious?**

I watch my phone, wait for the reply. It doesn't take long before it beeps.

He nicked a tractor off a farm and drove it off, Z was with him. Naughty naughty! Big

Rob's granddad saw them. Hee hee.

I put my phone down. I shake my head. I lie down on my bed and stare at the ceiling.

Zoë

My phone rings.

'Hello, Mum.'

'Hello, Zoë, love. Where are you? Are you all right?'

'I'm sitting on a wall, Mum, near the pier.'

'Are you OK, love? You sound sad. Is Gary there with you?'

I sigh. I look at the empty wall next to me. Gary isn't there. He's gone. I don't know where. Maybe I won't see him again. Maybe that's it. I feel like a complete bitch. 'I'm fine, Mum,' I say. 'Just a bit tired. Can you come and get me?'

'OK, love. We'll be there in a sec. Stay where you are.'

* * *

The journey starts with a big hug and a lot of tears, mine and Mum's. Then there are the questions. I give them a few answers. They don't believe me. That much is obvious. But I don't give everything away. I certainly don't tell them about the tractor and the gate and the fact that Gary's run away. I lie and tell them Gary's mum picked him up. When the questions are finished, Dad gives me the lecture. About how irresponsible it was. How I'd worried my mother and let's hope it hasn't had an effect on the unborn baby. How I should let them know where I'm going. All that stuff. It's silent for a bit, then. I stare out of the window. And everything goes rushing through my head again, all blurry like I'm standing in traffic, watching the headlights as the cars swerve around me.

Every field we go past, I think it's the one where we left the tractor. I keep looking for it, checking it's there, seeing if anyone's found it. But I think we must be going back a different way to the way Gary took us – the roads look much wider and busier. And I can't see the tractor.

Gary

I've been walking for a while now. There's a little lane with a sign. *Warston Beach 1/2 mile*, it says. I walk down the lane. I might as well. I might as well go somewhere. Otherwise I'll just keep walking.

The lane's really bendy. Seems to go on for ever. But after a few minutes there's an empty car park and a little bit further on there's some dunes. The beach must be on the other side of them. I walk straight past the car park and on to a little path that goes through the dunes. And straight away, I'm on to the beach. It's huge. The beach stretches as far as I can see on either side. And the sand goes out miles before it gets to the sea.

I sit down, look at the sea for a minute. But looking

at the sea makes me think about everything all over again. About the pier. About Zoë. About what I did. I hide my head away, in my arms. Only as soon as I do that I get a waft of Zoë off her flaming jumper. Oh, Jesus! I'm such an idiot.

I sit there, my head in my arms, and I just breathe. Try and concentrate on that instead of the other stuff. It's what Nan used to tell me to do if I was feeling angry. It feels like I'm doing it for ages, hours. But it don't really work, cos I'm still thinking all these thoughts. Every so often I convince myself that everything's OK really, that I'm overreacting, that I should go home. But it don't last long, cos then I think of me trying to kiss Zoë, or I think of the tractor, or Paul Knaggs, or my fucking mum and dad, or Henry's bloody gate, or the fucking medal man. Everything. It's all fucking wrong. I've messed it all up. There ain't no point going home. Most likely I'll get chucked out of school now I've hit Knaggs again. And now I've stolen a tractor, I'll probably be in trouble with the plod as well. They'll put me on a fucking ASBO or something. Give me a tag, so Paul Knaggs and all those bastards have got something else to take the mickey out of me for. So I ain't going back.

I don't know what I'm going to do, though. I could just walk straight out into the sea. Start walking into the water, and when it starts coming up around my ankles, my knees, my shoulders, my nose, my eyes, I would just keep walking until I'm completely underwater. I can't fucking swim, so I'd drown pretty bloody quick. Then that'd be it. No more problems. I wonder if it'd hurt when I ran out of oxygen, when the water started to flood into my mouth and my nose and my lungs.

I should do it. They'd be sorry then, sorry they treated me like shit. Mum would, definitely. She'd cry. Serve her right as well. I dunno about Dad. I s'pose he'd be upset. But he'd probably be pretty relieved as well, to have me out of the way. As for all the dicks at school, as for Paul Knaggs, I hope he'd feel so bloody guilty he'd top himself. I mean it. I hope he'd have such a guilty conscience that he couldn't live with it. I want him to know how it feels.

I dunno about Zoë. Maybe she'd be upset to start with, maybe she'd even cry. But she'd forget soon enough. She'd make some new friends or find some other div like me to help. After a year she'd forget who I was. She'd definitely be better off without me around.

David

I'm in bed. I should have been asleep ages ago. I was pretty tired earlier. But since Mum told me about Gary Wood, about his mum, well, now I can't relax. And Knaggs texting didn't help much, either. So I'm still awake. I don't feel like I could go to sleep at all. I feel kind of wired. You know, when I was really little and I couldn't sleep, I'd lie in bed and cry until someone came into my room. If it was Dad, he'd always joke that I must have a guilty conscience if I couldn't sleep. This time he'd be right. Cos I just keep thinking about what Mum said. And Knaggs's texts. I should have said something to Mum. I should have told her the truth.

See, if Wood has run away from home, if he's done

anything mental at all, it'll be my fault. Well, it'll be Knaggs's fault mostly. But I've just stood there like a pebblehead and let him do all this stuff to Wood. And I'm the one that keeps getting Knaggs off the hook. Like in the ICT room earlier. I should have done more. I should have stayed behind after the lesson and told Mr H what Knaggs had been up to. Stuff Knaggs. Stuff the rules.

I pick my phone up off the desk, go to my inbox and reread Knaggs's messages. I must've read them about 50 times already. Reading them again doesn't help.

I close my eyes and try to think of something else, something that'll stop me from thinking about Knaggs and Wood and me, something that'll get me to sleep. The first thing that pops into my brain is Zoë. I could think about me and Zoë being together, as unlikely as that sounds in real life. But it's what I've been thinking about most nights lately, if you know what I mean. I don't think it's a good idea right now, though. I don't think it'll help me sleep. So I start thinking about football instead: Norwich City in the final of the cup, which is probably even less likely to happen than me and Zoë getting together. But it might stop me from thinking about some of the other stuff.

Gary

It's freezing. Absolutely bloody freezing. My watch says 23:45. I'm still on the beach. Been here for hours now. Getting angry. Going mad. Freezing my bollocks off. Trying to think of what to do next. Where to go.

I'm feeling tired and I gotta find somewhere to sleep, somewhere a bit warmer than this stupid beach. I could walk back to East Strand, I s'pose. There are places in town I could sleep – shop doorways, beach huts and stuff. But I don't know if I wanna do that. I couldn't sleep in a doorway, with people going past, looking at me. I want somewhere a bit more private. I might be able to afford a shitty hotel or a B & B. I put my hand in my pocket, pull out my change and count it. £11.40 plus a few coppers. Won't be enough to stay anywhere, not even a shitty B & B. So I'll have to doss down.

I get up and brush the sand off my trousers, look both ways along the beach. I can't see anywhere that would be good for sleeping. I s'pose the other side of the dunes would be better, a bit more sheltered than the beach. So I go back through the dunes, along the path and on to the little lane again.

And I see the car park. There's a little building there. Toilets. All locked up. But I could force the door open. It'd be warmer than out here anyway. I walk over to it. And as I get closer the smell hits me. Piss. That's that. No way I'm going in there for the night. I'd rather freeze my arse off than have the smell of piss in my nose all night.

So I start walking again, through the car park. And at the end of the car park, I find a path that leads off, along the bottom of the dunes. So I follow it. The path's a bit overgrown with loads of thistles and stuff. But it's quite sheltered, with the dunes on one side and a hedge on the other. And it's warmer. I could sleep here, on the path, if the worst comes to the worst. Just tread the plants down a bit. But I keep walking, stepping on the thistles and the brambles and the nettles. Over the hedge I can see a field. There are cows in there, lying down at the other end. Guernseys.

Dad slept with the cows sometimes, when he worked for Henry. Not in a weird way. If they was calving or something. Or if they was ill. He'd set up a bed in the calving sheds. But I'm not gonna sleep in the field with them ones, that's for sure. So I keep walking.

After a while there are gardens on the other side of the hedge instead of fields. And that gives me an idea. Cos some of the gardens have got little sheds in them and stuff. The first two aren't big enough – I don't reckon I'd fit in them lying down. So I keep going. There ain't nothing in the next garden, just a kids' swing. But in the one after that, there's a boat. Quite a big boat, down at the end of the garden. I stop walking and look over the hedge. It's easily big enough to fit me in. It's got a cover over it as well. And there ain't no lights on in the house. None. No one's around. So I pull the hood of Zoë's jumper over my head and then squeeze through the hedge.

It's about one in the morning. I'm lying here, curled up in the bottom of the boat. Freezing. Uncomfortable. My mind's been rushing since I've been here, about what's happened, about what's gonna happen if I go back, about what I'm gonna do if I don't go back. But there's one thing that keeps coming back. Every time my brain feels like it's gonna explode with all the pressure, it comes into my head, like a little safety valve.

I've thought about it before. Before tonight, I mean. About topping myself. I've thought about it a few times. But then I could never do it. I never went as far as, like, slitting my wrists or nothing. But I thought about it. I thought about how I'd do it.

I know where I could get a gun. All I gotta do is go home and there's one waiting there. Dad don't use it no more, but he still keeps it. In the shed. It's a shotgun. One pull on the trigger and it's all over. I've thought about it a lot, lying here.

I saw this programme the other week on the telly, about this American kid. One day he took a gun to school. He'd been planning it for ages. He got hold of the gun from some dodgy shop or something and bought a load of ammo. Then he just went into school and started shooting: BANG, BANG, BANG. I've been thinking about that as well.

This American kid started off with all the kids he hated in school, all the ones that took the piss out of him and stuff. He lined them all up and then made them kneel down, made them beg for their lives, made them apologise for all the stuff they'd done. He even made them say some sick shit. Then he just shot them. BANG. Right in the middle of their foreheads, one after the other.

He done the same to the teachers. Well, most of them. Made them get down on their knees an' all.

Made them beg. Shot them. BANG.

After that he went mental, started shooting people at random. BANG, BANG, BANG, BANG.

In the end he ran out of bullets, ended up in the library, holding a load of other kids as hostages, ones he didn't really know. The police talked to him on a megaphone, tried to get him to let everyone go, started giving him some bullshit about how if he came out now it'd all be all right, they'd sort everything out. But he knew that was just a load of crap. Everything was messed up. Everyone'd messed him up and now he'd messed them up. And he knew he'd go to a prison for the rest of his life, getting even more shit. There was only one way that things was gonna get better. So he came running out of the school holding the gun, pretending like he was gonna shoot. Police shot him dead straight away.

Like I said, I've thought of that too. And I know who I'd kill first. I know what I'd make them say. I know how I'd kill them. And I know how I'd finish it. I'd save the last bullet for myself. BANG.

David

It's now three in the morning. The house is completely silent. I don't think I've slept at all. I've just been lying here, tossing and turning, trying not to think about stuff. But you know what it's like, trying not to think about stuff – your brain rebels and thinks about it even more. Or at least mine does.

I thought a change might help. So I got up a while back, poured a glass of milk and switched on the telly, started watching a repeat of an old American sitcom. I only watched it for about five minutes, though. I couldn't sit still. I couldn't concentrate. All I want to do is sleep, just blank everything out. I don't want to be lying here, thinking, feeling.

So I get up again and walk out of my bedroom. The landing's dark, but underneath Ollie's door I can see a crack of light. He's still up. And I can smell what he's doing. I knock on his door gently, so as not to wake Mum and Dad.

'What?' he says.

'It's me – David.'

After a few seconds the door swings open. The smell of spliff gets stronger. Ollie takes his spliff out of an ashtray, leans out of the window and takes a long drag.

'Why you still awake?' he says.

'Can't sleep.'

'Come and have a drag of this,' he says, holding out his spliff.

I shake my head. I can just imagine what Mum and Dad would do if they caught me smoking a spliff. They'd go absolutely mad. Like they did when they first caught Ollie. I go and sit down on his bed, though.

'Might help you relax . . .' he says.

I shake my head again.

Ollie shrugs and takes another drag. 'Suit yourself,' he says, after blowing the smoke out.

We sit there without speaking for a bit. There's some music playing really quietly. Some old, weird-sounding music.

'So, how come you can't sleep, then, Davey?' Ollie says.

I shrug my shoulders. 'Just can't. Can't stop

thinking about stuff.'

Ollie nods his head slowly. 'Thinking about what?' he says.

I look down at the carpet. 'Nothing important,' I say.

'You know what I do if I can't sleep?' Ollie says.

I look up again. I shake my head. 'What?'

'Mum's got some sleeping pills in the bathroom,' he says. 'Couple of them'll knock you out, no problem.'

'Really?'

Ollie nods. He picks up the spliff and carefully knocks the ash off the top of it.

'It's not dangerous, is it?' I say.

Ollie takes another drag. He shakes his head. He blows out the smoke. 'It's fine,' he says, kind of gasping the words out. 'They wouldn't be allowed to make them otherwise.'

So I go into the bathroom. Switch the light on, go over to the medicine cabinet, open it. I have to rummage through it – there's loads of stuff in there, most of it out of date. The sleeping pills are right at the back behind the aspirin and the paracetamol. I read the bottle. Two tablets to be taken before bed. I undo the lid, shake the tablets out, and then gulp them down with a mouthful of water. I put the tablets where I found them and then return to my room. I puff up the pillows, straighten my duvet and get in. Close my eyes and take a deep breath, wait for sleep to come.

THURSDAY

Gary

It starts getting light early. I haven't slept too well. I don't think I've slept at all, to be honest. Too much stuff going through my head. Too angry. Too embarrassed. Too everything. So as soon as the birds start singing and the sun's out, I get out of the boat and stretch. My back and my shoulders feel stiff. But I don't hang about. I don't want no one from the house to see me and call the police. So I squeeze back through the hedge on to the path and I start walking. Back towards the car park.

There's a car in it already. I look at my watch. It's only half past five. Who goes to the beach at that time? I walk along the path, through the dunes. The sound of the waves hits me straight away. It's really loud. It wakes me up. And the air as well. It's wet and cold and salty and fresh.

I walk along the beach, kick a few stones, look out at the sea. There are some ships sitting on the horizon. They're not really moving. Maybe they're anchored, waiting to go into the harbour along the coast. Or maybe they're just going very slowly. I'm not sure. I don't really know much about boats.

I'm thinking about what I'm gonna do. What I'm gonna do with the rest of my life. I could just start walking. I could go anywhere. Scotland, maybe. If I walked for ten, twenty miles a day, it'd take me a couple of months, I think. Or I could steal a car. I've never driven a car before, but I s'pose it can't be that different from a tractor. I could get a job somewhere, on a farm or something, find somewhere to live. I reckon I'd be better off than I am right now.

A little further up the beach I can see a load of stuff that's washed ashore, probably off a boat or something. When I was little and Nan used to take me to the beach, sometimes we'd find stuff that'd floated all the way from Holland washed up on the shore. I walk towards all the crap. There's a load of nets and some wood, a bit of seaweed. But I can see something quite big and red as well. Looks like a buoy from a distance. But when I get up close, I can see it's not a buoy. It's a petrol can. I pick it up and look at it. It's empty. There ain't no holes in it as far as I can see.

And then I have an idea. So I turn round and head back up the beach with the can. And I feel a bit better. I think I know what I'm gonna do. I think I know how I'm gonna make things right.

David

I get woken up at seven o'clock by my phone. Another bloody text. I sit up in bed. It's wet – feels like I've pissed the bed. But it's just sweat. I must have got into a really deep sleep after the sleeping pills. My mouth feels dry. My head feels fuzzy.

I get out of bed and grab my phone. I know who the text's gonna be from before I even look. Knaggs. And when I do look, I'm right.

Davey, have u got a toy tractor? I can feel some piss-takin comin on!

I sigh, run my hand through my hair. I stare at the text for a while. I press 'Reply' on my phone and start to text. **No, I haven't. Stop being a dick** is as far as I get before I press the red button on my phone and save the message as a draft instead of sending it.

I lie back on my bed. But it's cold and wet and smells of sweat. So I sit straight back up again. And I stare into space. My head feels weird. I've got this feeling in my stomach, like I've done something wrong, like I should be doing something to put it right. I sit there for ages.

There's a knock on my door. It opens and Mum looks in. 'Oh, you are up then,' she says. 'Come on, David. It's a quarter past seven. You need to get a move on or you'll be late.'

I don't move. I can hear her, but I'm still staring into space, still thinking and feeling rubbish. I see her take a step into my room.

'Are you OK, David?' she says.

I sit there for a few seconds and stare. I nod my head. Mum looks at me like she's trying to work out if I really am OK. But then she turns and walks back out of my room, clumps downstairs.

I don't want to get up. I don't want to go downstairs and eat breakfast. I don't want to go to school. I just want to stay in my bedroom all day. I want to stay out of Knaggs's way, out of everyone's way.

But Mum calls from downstairs, 'Come on, David!

Your breakfast's on the table!'

I get up and put my dressing gown on. And I go down to breakfast.

Zoë

I'm sitting at the breakfast table, unable to swallow my mouthful of cornflakes, as Mum and Dad look at me and make concerned faces.

'Is everything all right, Zoë?' Mum says. 'You look worried.'

I don't look at her. I couldn't say anything even if I wanted to, with a mouthful of soggy cornflakes.

'Come on, love, you can tell me,' she says. 'Is it something at school that's worrying you?'

I shake my head.

'Is it the tramp?'

I shake my head again.

'The move?'

I shake my head.

Mum sighs. Then she puts her hand on my arm. I look at her. She smiles. 'Zoë, sometimes it helps to share a problem. Just telling someone else can make the problem seem less important.'

I smile at her, my mouth still full of cornflakes. And then I get up from the table, go to the bathroom and spit the cornflakes into the toilet.

I'm sitting on my bed. I can't stop thinking about Gary, wondering about what happened to him after he walked off. I hope he calmed down a bit, went home. I really hope that's what he did. But even though I want to think that's what happened, I know it probably isn't. I bet he didn't go home last night. I bet he slept rough somewhere, like a field or a barn or something. Right now, he'll be trying to get as far away as possible from everyone. Either that or he's being pulled out of the sea or something *really* stupid. But I can't think about that. He wouldn't do that. I hope.

I pick up my phone. I open 'My contacts', go to Gary's number. My thumb's poised above the green button. One press and it'll dial the number. Ask one question and I can find out if Gary went home last night. But I'm not sure I can do it. I close my eyes, take a deep breath and force my thumb to press the button. Then I hold the phone to my ear.

It rings.

Again.

And again.

And again.

'Hello?' It's a woman's voice. It must be Gary's mum. She sounds sort of desperate.

And I go mute. I can't make my mouth say any words. I don't know what to say to her. I can't just ask her whether Gary came home last night. If he didn't come back, this is gonna upset her even more. I shouldn't have phoned.

'Hello?' she says again. 'Is anyone there? Is that you, Gary? Where are you?'

Crap! I knew it. He didn't come home last night.

'Hello?' she says again. Now she sounds angry. She sighs, swears under her breath, and the line goes dead.

I sit there and stare into space. He's gone. I'll never see him again. And it's my fault.

I walk really slowly to the bus stop. All the way there I'm thinking that if I happen to get there too late and the bus is already gone, then I have a legitimate excuse not to go to school. Then maybe I could go and look for Gary, make things right. But when I get to the bus stop, the bus is there and people are getting on it.

'All right, Zoë?' Knaggs says. 'Did you have a nice time yesterday?' He smirks at me.

'What?'

He laughs. 'You weren't at school yesterday. Did you go anywhere nice?' Knaggs looks at me. He looks like he knows something and he can't wait to say it. But there's no way he can know about last night.

'Get lost, Paul,' I say. And I start to walk towards the bus.

Knaggs walks after me. 'No sign of the cheese-puff boy this morning, Zoë,' he says. 'Did you find him in the end? Had he topped himself? Is that why you've got a face like a slapped arse?'

'Go away!' I say to him. And I get on the bus and sit as far away from him as I can.

Gary

I put the petrol can on the counter. A bottle of water and a pasty as well.

The man in the petrol station looks at me funny, suspicious. But all he says is, 'Pump number five?'

I nod my head. 'Yeah,' I say. 'Can I have a box of matches too?'

He nods, turns round and gets a matchbox. I know what he's thinking. He thinks I'm gonna set fire to something. Well, maybe he's right. I haven't decided yet. He scans the other stuff through. 'Ten ninety-eight,' he says.

I give him the money.

He fiddles about in the till and hands my change

over. He looks at me funny again. But he still doesn't say nothing.

I turn away and get out of there as quick as I can.

I walk along the side of the road. It's still early – just after seven – but the roads are starting to fill up with cars. When I'm out of sight of the petrol station I stop and rip open the pasty. I take a bite. It's too cold. It don't taste of nothing. But I'm hungry as a bloody bear, so it'll have to do. I take a swig of water and start walking again.

The walk takes about half an hour into East Strand and then back out the other side. And when I get to the field, it's still there. Henry's tractor. I look along the road, make sure no one's watching. There isn't anyone about, so I open the gate. And I walk back over to the tractor.

I pour diesel into the tractor's tank, put the top back on the can and chuck it in the tractor cab. I climb in after it and take the keys out of my pocket. I nearly threw them in the sea last night, when I was angry. I sigh. Put the key in and start up the tractor. It doesn't start first time. It wouldn't, would it? But the second time it does and I drive it out of the field and on to the road.

David

I'm in a kind of daze. My head feels like someone's taken my brain out and put some polystyrene in there instead. I can't think straight. Maybe it's cos I'm tired. Or maybe it's cos of the sleeping pills.

I go and stand by the chicken-wire fence, throw my bag down and just stare into space, wishing I was somewhere else other than school.

After a while, Knaggs comes into the playground. He walks over to me, throws his bag so that it skids along the playground until it crashes into the fence. He smiles. 'All right, Davey-Dave?'

I nod at him. 'All right.' I don't want to talk to him. I want him to go away. But I can't say that to him.

'Hey, what about Wood?' he says. He looks at me expectantly, with this excited expression on his face.

I look away from him, at the ground. 'What about him?'

'You got my texts, didn't you?' Knaggs says. 'Stupid Farmer Boy stole a tractor, with Zoë!'

I kick a stone around the playground. It gives me a reason to have my head down, to avoid looking at Knaggs. 'I know,' I say. 'So what?'

Knaggs keeps following me around. He obviously can't take the hint that I don't want to speak to him. 'Well, Davey-Dave,' he says, 'Zoë was on the bus this morning but there was no sign of Farmer Boy. Do you reckon the cops caught him? He might be in a cell right now! What sentence do you think they give tramp-murdering tractor thieves? Life? The death penalty?'

I stop kicking the stone and look at Knaggs. He's smiling. And something – maybe his smirking face, maybe what he's saying, maybe lack of sleep – makes me snap. My heart starts beating like mad, and before I know it, I'm right in Knaggs's face. 'He's missing!' I say. 'No one knows where he is. He's run away from home. His mum's crying. Is that funny?'

Knaggs stares back at me. He seems shocked.

I take a step back. I can't look at Knaggs any more.

'Jesus, calm down!' Knaggs says. And then, after a

while, he says, 'How d'you know all that?'

I sigh. 'Because my mum told me. Because she's had Wood's mum on the phone to her in tears, asking what to do.'

'Shit!' Knaggs says. 'Shit!'

We both stand by the fence, not talking to each other for ages.

'Have they called the police?' Knaggs says.

I shake my head. 'Not yet.' And then I pick up my bag and look for somewhere else to stand.

Gary

It feels weird, driving this tractor on the road. Like I'm gonna get caught or something. I didn't think about it yesterday. It just seemed like the right thing to do. But it's making me nervous right now.

I have to do this, though. I've got to go back. There's stuff that needs sorting out. There isn't any other way for everything to work out right. I just want to be there. I want this to be over.

I go back the same way I drove yesterday. Quiet roads, no cars, no houses, no people. I don't see another human being. It's a good job as well, cos I'm so shitted up, so on edge, that I think if I did, I'd have a heart attack or something. But when I get to just outside Wallingham, instead of turning off towards Henry's farm, I just keep going. And then my heart starts to beat really fast. I'm really gonna do this. I'm gonna get my own back on Paul Knaggs. I'm gonna finish this.

I stop just outside Wendham, park Henry's pile-of-shit tractor in a field that looks like no one's been there for months – years, maybe. I grab my stuff out of the tractor – bottle, petrol can, matches, keys. And I jump out of the cab. There's a tap in the field. I stop by it and fill up. Then I walk into Wendham.

My hands are sweaty. My heart's beating like bloody mad. I can feel it right up in my throat. I feel sick. But I keep walking. Ten more minutes and this'll be over. Ten more minutes of feeling like this, then it's done, no going back. A minute later and I'm in the village. Wendham. I hate this place. Nothing good's ever happened to me here. I walk past the school and my heartbeat gets even faster, like my chest's gonna burst open all over the pavement. I take a swig out of my bottle and I try and take a couple of deep breaths. I walk past the school to the church and into the churchyard.

I crouch down by the churchyard wall. I can see the playground from here. Kids are in there already, standing around in their stupid little groups, taking the piss out of each other, chatting away about nothing. I just crouch there, petrol can in one hand, bottle of water in the other. And I watch them and wait for the right time.

I start to feel calm, crouched there. More calm than I was a few minutes ago, anyway. I know that I'm gonna do it now. I know that I'm not gonna chicken out.

I have to wait a few minutes before I see who I'm looking for. Paul Knaggs. He walks into the playground and chucks his bag down by the fence. Then he stands there, with David. He's the one that stitched me up to Mr Moore, David is – I'm sure. Knaggs and David start talking. After a few seconds, David tries to walk away from Knaggs. But Knaggs follows him, still talking. And after a while, David steps right up into Knaggs's face, like he's gonna hit him or something. He says something to him, can't hear what, though. And then he backs off. They say a few more things to each other, then David grabs his bag and walks away from Knaggs.

Knaggs walks off as well. Over to Zoë. He kind of follows her about. He looks like he's pretending to drive a car or something. Zoë turns. She looks pissed off. But he just laughs, says something. Then she walks off, looking angry.

I give it a few more seconds, wait till Knaggs is

definitely on his own. And I jump the wall. I walk straight over to him. And I feel really strong, like I could rip off his head if I wanted. But I'm not going to. I just stand in front of him with the petrol can in my hand, wait for him to see me. Wait for him to take the bait.

He laughs. 'All right, Gary?' he says. 'What you got there? You been filling up your tractor? I thought you'd run away from home! Hey, is that a girl's hoodie you're wearing?'

'You think you're pretty funny, don't you?'

Knaggs nods his head. 'Yeah, I am. Funnier than you, anyway.'

I don't say anything. I'm feeling weird. My head's swimming. I don't know whether I can go through with this.

Knaggs smirks at me.

And I know I have to do something. Or else it'll just be like it was before. Him in control, taking the piss. So I do it. I slowly unscrew the lid of the petrol can and then hold the can up in front of me.

The smirk on Knaggs's face goes. He stares at the petrol can. He looks scared, freaked out.

I smile at him.

'What are you doing?' he says. He sounds serious now.

I start pouring the contents of the can on to the

ground. Some lands on Knaggs's trainers. He's shitting himself. I'm in control. 'Whoops!' I say. 'Sorry, I slipped.' And I smile.

Knaggs looks at his shoe and he looks at me. 'What the fuck are you doing?' he says. 'Psycho!'

I pull the box of matches from my pocket. I rattle them and watch Knaggs's face. The colour has drained away.

'Is that petrol in there?' he says, pointing to the can.

'No.' I shake my head. 'It's diesel.'

His eyes are going bulgy now. You can see that he's thinking about what to do. Should he run? Should he shout for help? Or should he stand there and let me do it, pretend like he's a real man?

I spill a bit more out of the can, on to his trousers.

'Stop it!' he says.

'Say you're sorry or I'll pour the lot on you and light a match!' I say.

'What the fuck?' Knaggs says.

'You heard. Say you're sorry!'

He's panicking now. He thinks he might die. He doesn't know what to do. 'I'm sorry,' he says. But he doesn't sound that sorry to me. Not sorry enough.

'Beg me to forgive you.'

He looks round. People are watching us. There's a crowd of people gathering. I need to do this soon, before someone jumps on me and stops me.

'Get back!' I shout at the crowd. I let some more dribble out of the petrol can on to the ground, so everyone gets back. I turn to Knaggs. 'Say it!'

He looks at the ground. 'Will you forgive me?' he says quietly.

'Louder!' I say.

'Will you forgive me?' he says again, a little louder.

The crowd's getting closer again. So I stare at them. It doesn't take much to make them move back – they all think I'm mental already.

I turn back to Knaggs. 'Say you're a dickhead!'

Knaggs looks at me. For a second there's a little smile on his face. 'You're a dickhead!' he says.

The crowd laugh a little. Till I look at them and let even more spill out of the can.

'That wasn't a good idea, Paul,' I say. I step towards him, pour more over him.

He starts to shake. He's petrified.

'Say you're a dickhead!' I say.

'I'm a dickhead,' he says quietly.

I smile. I take a match from the box, and the crowd moves back. Cowards. They won't even step in and save him.

'Please don't,' Knaggs says. He's staring at the match.

'Don't what?'

'Don't do it! I'm sorry. I won't take the piss out of

you again. Just don't do it!'

I smile at him. Slosh a bit more out of the can. I walk straight past him, barge him out the way, letting the rest of the liquid dribble out of the can. Then I turn and throw the can at him. And I light the match.

He stares at me. There are a million things going through his head. I can see it in his eyes. Now he knows how it feels. I drop the match. He closes his eyes before it hits the trail of liquid.

'BANG!'

PART THREE

David

The match fizzles out as soon as it hits the ground.

I just stand there and stare at it.

Everyone does, too shocked to move or say anything, trying to work out what on earth just happened. Everyone except Wood. He must have run off, cos when I look up he's not there any more. No one's stopped him. He's gone, as quick as he came.

Knaggs lies there on the ground, in the puddle of petrol or whatever it is. He's shaking. He looks absolutely terrified. I'm not surprised. I am too.

Because I'm his best friend, I should be the one that goes and helps him up. I should probably run after Wood and fight him for Knaggs. It's the kid rules: you stand up for your mates. No matter how much of a pebblehead they've been, no matter how much you realise you don't like them. But fuck the rules. I'm not going to go and pick Knaggs up and see if he's OK. I let someone else go over instead. Mikey and George.

Out of the corner of my eye, I can see Zoë. She walks closer. She stands near me. She looks over at Knaggs. I wonder if she saw what happened, saw what Wood did? She stares at Knaggs like he's nothing, like he's worse than a piece of shit that she's found on the bottom of her shoe. Then she storms off. I think about going after her. But before I can make my mind up, she's out of sight. I turn back, stare at Knaggs.

Knaggs stares back. Not just at me, but at everyone who's gawping at him. He's stopped shaking now. He doesn't look scared any more, just really angry and embarrassed. 'What you looking at?' he shouts.

Most people move away from him, chatting and laughing. But I just stand there. And Knaggs walks over, towards me.

'Shit!' he says. 'What was all that about?'

I shake my head. 'Dunno,' I say. 'You all right?'

He looks down at his soaked trousers and trainers. 'Jesus!'

'You all right?'

'You can be my witness,' he says. 'You saw all that, didn't you?'

I nod.

'I'm gonna get that psycho put in prison for this! He tried to kill me!'

I look blankly back at Knaggs. I'm still trying to work out what happened. It can't have been petrol in the can. Otherwise it would have gone straight up. Knaggs should be dead. Wood was just trying to put the shits up Knaggs. I smile to myself. Just for a second.

'Come on,' Knaggs says. 'Let's go and see Mr Moore. We'll finally get the cheese-puff boy thrown out of school for this.' He starts walking towards the school, but I don't follow him. After a few steps, he stops and looks round at me. 'What you doing, Davey-boy?' he says. 'You saw it. He's dangerous! Come on, you're my star witness.'

I stare at him. It's my duty as his best friend to lie for him, to cover his back, like I did before. But I can't do it. Not again. I shake my head.

'I didn't see anything, Knaggs,' I say.

Knaggs looks at me, half confused, half annoyed. 'What?'

'I didn't see anything,' I say. 'Apart from Wood splashing a bit of water on you. And you getting all hysterical. That's all I saw.'

Knaggs walks straight up to me, gets right in my face. 'What did you say?'

'You heard,' I say. 'There's nothing to tell Mr Moore. You got scared by a bit of water and acted like a pebblehead. The end.'

I walk away from him. My heart's beating like mental. I can't believe I just said that.

'You're a twat, David,' Knaggs shouts after me. 'Find yourself a new friend.'

But I just keep walking. I want to find Zoë.

Zoë

I'm walking away from the playground towards the skanky mobile classrooms. I'm glad Gary's OK, I'm glad he's alive, I'm glad he came back. But what just happened? That was scary. Maybe I should have gone after him. Maybe I should have made sure that he didn't do anything stupid to himself. Or to anyone else. I definitely don't think he knows what he's doing any more.

'Zoë!' a voice calls from behind me.

I turn. It's David – one of Knaggs's mates. I stop walking. 'What?' I say angrily. 'What do you want?'

He looks down at the ground. He looks uncomfortable. Maybe he's not just gonna take the mickey. 'Can

I talk to you?' he says quietly. And he looks up at me. He looks upset. I keep expecting him to smirk, like Knaggs would. But he doesn't. He keeps looking at me, like a scared little kid or something.

I don't know what to do. I don't know whether to trust him. This could all be part of a wind-up. But then what do I have to lose? Things can't get much worse than they already are. 'OK,' I say. 'Why not?'

'Not here,' he says. 'Somewhere quiet. Come on – there are some benches near the field.'

So I follow him, past the mobile classrooms, past the music block, to the benches near the field. We sit down next to each other. He doesn't look at me. He's gone really pale. He looks like I feel.

'So what is it?' I say.

'It's Knaggs,' David says. 'And Wood.'

'Right,' I say. I look out across the field. 'Look, can you just give Gary a break? I know what he did was stupid, but, you know, he's going through a bad time . . .'

'I know,' David says. 'That's why I needed to talk to you.'

I look at David. He's nervous. 'What do you mean?' I say.

He takes a deep breath. 'I have to help him,' he says. 'Gary, I mean.'

I still expect him to smirk, for this to be a joke. But he sits there, looking down at his feet as he taps them on the ground.

'Are you serious?'

He nods his head.

'But I thought Paul Knaggs was your best friend,' I say.

David looks at me. 'He *was*,' he says.

And I think he's being serious. 'There's not much we can do now, though. Is there?' I say. 'It's already gone way too far.'

'I know,' David says. 'But I have to do something. This is my fault.'

I shake my head. 'He's gonna get chucked out of school for good, isn't he? For bringing a petrol can and some matches into school and threatening someone. That's serious. They could bring the police in for that.'

David sighs. He stops tapping his feet. 'Knaggs has gone to see Mr Moore,' he says.

I shake my head. That's it. Gary's gone. He's completely messed it up for himself. He'll get chucked out of school. Maybe that's what he wanted.

'Will you come with me and see Mr Moore? I want to tell him what's been going on. I want to tell him all the stuff that Knaggs has done.'

I look up at him. He really does seem upset. But I'm

still not sure if I can trust him. I half expect Paul Knaggs to jump out and laugh at me for believing this. 'Do you mean it? You're gonna grass on Knaggs?'

David takes a deep breath. 'I have to,' he says. He stands up. 'Please.'

I get up as well. 'Come on, then.'

Gary

I walk out of Wendham, to the field, get back in the tractor and drive out of there as quickly as I can. I'm shaking. I feel sick. What I just did was sick. I can't believe that I did it. I went too far. They all thought I was mad before – now they're gonna know it. They'll lock me up and throw away the key. Knaggs thought he was gonna die, thought that there was petrol or something in the can. I could see it in his eyes. Fear. He was almost crying. And I made him feel like that. It was me. I'm sick. Messed up in the head. Wrong.

Knaggs will be in with Mr Moore now. They'll be fussing over him and he'll be pretending to be a poor innocent little boy, pretending like butter wouldn't melt in his mouth. And he'll have all his bloody mates backing him up, saying what a psycho I am. I shouldn't have done it. I should have just kept running, as far away from this place as I can get.

I have to stop a few times on the road back to Wallingham to let cars past. They all look at me funny. They can probably see I'm not old enough to be driving a tractor. But I don't really care any more. They can phone the cops for all I care. They'll already be after me for what I've just done. And for stealing the tractor in the first place. Doesn't make any difference what I do now. I can't get into any more trouble than I'm already in.

After a while, I get close to Wallingham. I take a left to go around the outside of the village. God knows how I've managed to get all the way back here. I must have put my foot on the accelerator and changed gears and all that, but I don't remember doing it.

Before long, I can see Henry's farmhouse. There's still police tape around it. I drive straight past it and then take a right at the crossroads, keep going till I get to the gate I busted through yesterday and into the field. I take the tractor back into the farmyard, park it up in the barn, where it was before. As though nothing's happened, as though it's been here all along.

I switch the engine off, but I don't get out of the tractor. I just sit there, staring. And everything rushes through my head – millions of thoughts and feelings and voices. I can't stop them.

David

I look at Zoë. She looks back at me. She smiles. She looks about as nervous as I am.

I feel dizzy and sick. Maybe this isn't the right thing to do. The kid rules are there for a reason – they must be. You should never grass on your mates. Maybe I should say nothing, do nothing, and just make sure that I stay well away from Knaggs from now on.

We keep walking through the corridor. There's hardly anyone inside, cos the bell still hasn't gone, just a few teachers rushing about, carrying piles of photocopying and stuff.

We stop outside the glass door of the school office. Zoë knocks on the door. Mrs Wilson, Mr Moore's secretary, calls us in. Zoë opens the door and we walk up to Mrs Wilson's desk.

'Yes,' she says. 'What can I do for you?'

I look at Zoë. I don't want to be the one to speak.

'We need to see Mr Moore,' she says. 'Urgently.'

Mrs Wilson makes a face, raises her eyebrows. 'He's in a meeting with another student at the moment,' she says. 'He can't be disturbed. Could you come back later, or would you like me to give him a message?'

Zoë looks really worried. She leans towards the desk a little. 'It's really important,' she says. 'I need to see him. It's about what happened in the playground earlier. It's about Paul Knaggs and Gary Wood.'

'Oh, I see,' says Mrs Wilson. 'Right. If you have a seat on the green chairs over there, I'll let him know that you're here.'

Gary

I don't know how long I've been sitting here, on this tractor, in this barn. But it must be ages. I jump down from the tractor and walk out of Henry's poxy barn, back out into the field. I walk straight across it, kicking the long grass, stamping it down, all the way across to the gate. It isn't as busted as I thought it'd be after I smashed through it. It's come off its hinges and it's a tiny bit dented. Chain's broken as well. But nothing that can't be fixed.

I walk past the fence and out on to the road. I cross the road and go up on to the verge on the other side. I climb the fence and look into the field. It's Michael Yaxton's field. He's a miserable old man. All he grows is oilseed rape. It bloody stinks. I jump over his fence and walk along the tractor tracks at the edge of the field. Right at the end of Yaxton's field, there's another fence. I climb over it and I'm on to the track that runs down to the back of our shitty house. I walk down the track as far as our back garden. Have a look around. No one's watching. I know what I've got to do, what I have to get. And I don't have to go into the house to get it. Only into the shed in the garden. Which is just as well, cos I reckon if I did go into the house, I'd get an earful, a load of grief and a load of questions. And I don't need that. So I squeeze through the hedge quietly, keeping my eyes on the back of the house, making sure that no one sees me. I walk over to the shed, open the door and I'm in.

The shed's a mess. It's where Dad keeps all his rubbish. His tools, his beer, his porno mags. And his gun. Stupid idiot don't even have a lock on it. The cops would have him for that if they ever found out.

David

We sit on the green chairs for ages. I feel sick with guilt and nerves. Not just about what I'm gonna say and what's happened, but also because of what people will think if they see me waiting to see Mr Moore. They'll know I'm about to grass on my best mate. My old best mate, anyway. Cos that's what's happening here. I might as well be signing my own death warrant. Once I do this, my life in this school will be over. Knaggs will see to that. I'll be sat with the pebbleheads in lessons. And in the dinner hall. I'll have to sit near the front of the school bus. I'll even have to change where I hang my stuff up in the changing rooms. Cos once this is done, I'll be a nobody.

The bell for the start of school goes while me and Zoë are sitting on the green chairs. We're missing registration. I'd much rather be there right now, answering my name, than here. But this is my choice. This is what I have to do.

We don't say a word to each other, Zoë and me. Mrs Wilson sits at her desk and answers the phone, takes some messages, makes some phone calls, looks at her computer. Above her head, on the wall, there's a clock. It's five past nine now. Feels like we've been sitting here for ages. Quarter of an hour.

But then Mr Moore's office door opens. Knaggs steps out with Mr Moore.

'Thanks for coming to see me, Paul,' Mr Moore says. 'Go to class now. I'll find you if I need to talk to you again.'

Knaggs walks out. He looks up and he sees me sitting on the green chairs. And my heart starts racing, thumping against my chest. I can feel my cheeks going red. He looks straight back at me, daggers in his eyes. He knows why I'm here. I'll be a dead man walking before I even get to class. If Mr Moore wasn't here right now, Knaggs would go for me in a second. He walks across the room and opens the glass door. He turns and looks at me again and shakes his head. And then he leaves.

'David, Zoë,' says Mr Moore. 'Come in.'

'Sit down, please,' Mr Moore says.

I sink into the soft chair but I sit up straight.

'Are you all right, Zoë?' says Mr Moore. 'I had a phone call from the police yesterday.'

Zoë looks surprised. Her cheeks go red. 'What? Really? Why?' she says.

'They told me that you and Gary Wood had found a body,' says Mr Moore. He looks really serious. 'It must be quite a shock to find someone like that. If you need to talk to anyone, just say.'

'Oh,' says Zoë. She sounds kind of relieved. 'Yeah. No, I'm fine about that.'

'Well, we're here if you need to talk, Zoë, really we are,' Mr Moore says. 'Anyway, Mrs Wilson tells me that you two saw what happened in the playground this morning.'

I nod. So does Zoë.

Mr Moore sighs. He shifts in his chair, looks right at Zoë first, then at me. 'I want you both to know that I'm taking this incident very seriously indeed. You need to realise that I can't guarantee that anything you tell me will remain confidential. I don't know where this matter will go just yet, but I may have to relay anything you tell me to the police. You understand that, don't you?'

I nod.

'The police?' says Zoë. She looks angry. 'Why are they involved?'

'They aren't,' Mr Moore says. 'Yet. But from what Paul Knaggs has said, this is a very serious matter. I wouldn't be at all surprised if the police did become involved.'

Zoë stares at Mr Moore angrily, like she's gonna get up and storm out or something. I just look down at the floor. I don't know why I thought this was a good idea, coming in here. There isn't anything we can do. It's too late – I've left it too late. Wood took it too far.

'So, what did you see?' Mr Moore says calmly.

Next to me, Zoë takes a deep breath. 'We need to talk to you about Gary,' she says. 'It wasn't his fault, what happened today . . .'

Mr Moore breathes in deeply through his nostrils. 'I see,' he says. 'Go ahead then.'

Zoë looks across at me. I meet her eyes for a second or two, but then I have to look away, down at the floor. I have no idea what to say. There's nothing that I can say. I've made a mistake. I shouldn't have come in here. I can't help.

Zoë looks back at Mr Moore. 'Paul Knaggs has been bullying Gary, sir,' she says. 'Even I can see that, and I've only been here a week. He won't leave him alone. Paul pushed him to do this.'

Mr Moore raises an eyebrow. 'Really? How?'

Zoë looks at me again. But I have nothing to say. I

look away, at my shoes. I wipe my clammy hands on my trousers.

'He does it all the time. On the bus. In lessons. In Wallingham,' Zoë says.

'How? How does he bully Gary?' Mr Moore says.

I'm not sure he believes her.

Zoë sighs. 'He just says things all the time. He calls him "Farmer Boy" and "the cheese-puff boy". The other day he told everyone that Gary had murdered a tramp, after . . .' Zoë's voice trails off.

Mr Moore nods. 'I see,' he says. He picks up his notebook from the table and writes something down.

'And he said this stuff about how he wants Gary to be dead,' Zoë says.

Mr Moore puts his notebook down. He leans forward. 'Really?'

Zoë nods. She takes a couple of deep breaths.

'When? To who?'

'To me . . . a few times,' Zoë says.

Mr Moore leans back in his chair again. He looks up at the ceiling, runs his hands through his hair, like he's thinking. Then he looks back at Zoë and me. 'What exactly did he say?' Mr Moore says.

Zoë doesn't say anything straight away. The phone rings in the office outside. The clock on the wall ticks. 'I can't remember exactly,' she says. 'But yesterday, I went looking for Gary after school and I saw Paul

Knaggs on his way back from the bus stop. I asked him where Gary was and he said that Gary had probably killed himself. He said once before that he hoped Gary was dead.'

Mr Moore sighs. He raises his eyebrows. He picks his notebook up off his desk again. 'OK,' he says. He pauses. I don't think he knows what to say. 'Do you know why he said that?'

Zoë shakes her head. 'I don't know,' she says. 'I wasn't at school yesterday. But something happened, I think.'

It's quiet again for a few seconds. Just the ticking of the clock, the squeak as Mr Moore moves in his chair. Then he sighs and sits forward again. 'How about you, David? Were you at school yesterday?'

I can hear my heartbeat in my temples. I can feel it in my ears. I look up at Mr Moore. 'Yes,' I say. It comes out like a croak.

'Do you know what happened yesterday? Do you know why Paul might have said that about Gary?'

They're both looking at me. Mr Moore and Zoë. I look back at Mr Moore, cos I can't look at Zoë. I can tell that her eyes are begging me to tell him, to make this all right. And I don't know if I can do it. I don't know. I take a couple of breaths, try and stay calm. And I open my mouth.

'Yeah,' I say. 'Yeah, I know what happened.'

Gary

I grab what I need out of the shed, put the gun over my shoulder and sneak back through the hedge. No one sees me. Mum and Dad probably haven't even noticed I didn't come home yesterday. They might think I'm still at school. Except Paul Knaggs has probably gone squealing to the teachers by now. The school will have phoned Mum.

I check along the track. No one's around. I run across the track and over the fence, into Yaxton's field. And then I keep walking, till I'm well away from the track. I sit down. Check the gun out. It's seen better days. Dad used to take good care of it, used to clean it and oil it after he'd finished with it. But he don't any more. He hardly uses it. It still smells of the oil, though. It makes me think of when I was little, when Dad used to clean his gun in the kitchen. I used to sit at the table and watch him. But he wouldn't let me help him. Said it was too dangerous. But I used to like the smell of the oil.

I empty the stuff out of the front pocket of Zoë's jumper. Screwdriver, wrench, hammer, Zoë's bloody bubble blower. And some cartridges for the gun, four of them, red ones. I take two of the cartridges, load them into the chamber of the gun and then snap it shut. All I need to do is point it at my head and pull the trigger and it'll stop. All of it. For ever. No one would be able to get me then. There's no way I could survive it. But I keep the barrel of the gun pointed away from me, put the other cartridges and the stuff back in the pocket of the jumper and stand up.

I walk further up the field, till I'm level with the gate into Henry's field on the other side of the road. I check the road. There's a car coming, a blue metro van – old Victor's van. So I duck down and wait for it to go past. He takes ages. That van'll only go about ten mile an hour. When he's past, I leave it a few seconds, then check the road again. No cars. So I jump the fence and then race across the road, into Henry's field.

I put the gun down near the hedge, so no one will see it. I get the tools out of the pocket and try to mend

Henry's stupid bloody gate. I haven't mended one before. I helped Dad put one up in another field once. It isn't easy on my own, though. See, when I hung the gate with Dad, one of us held each end, so we could get it level and lift it on to the frame properly. But when I pick it up on my own, I stumble about all over the place, nearly break my bloody neck as I fall backwards. It takes a couple of goes to lift it on to the frame. I can't find the nuts to fasten it on, so it'll just have to do as it is. It won't fall off, anyway. I've made something right. It doesn't look like it's been bust any more.

I walk over to the hedge and pick up Dad's gun. I turn and walk quickly across the field to the barn, cos I don't want anyone to see me. The sun's just coming out from behind the clouds. It's pretty warm. It's nearly summertime. There are flowers in among all the grass and nettles and brambles in the field. Poppies mostly, but there's others as well. I don't know their names, though. And there are loads of birds singing. A cuckoo, some blackbirds, robins, a skylark.

I don't go into the barn. It's still shady in there. I sit against the wall instead, on some overgrown grass, in the sunshine. I put the gun down next to me and I shut my eyes, let my head fall back so that it rests against the crumbly bricks of the barn. I put my head in my hands and take some deep breaths. I can feel tears forming behind my eyes. I bite my bottom lip, try and stop myself from crying. But the tears start to come anyway, start to leak from my eyes and run down my face. I try to fight them, try to stop them, but I can't. They just keep coming and I start sobbing. And I keep thinking, Why's all this shit happened to me? How come I'm the one who finds a dead body? How come I'm the one who gets the piss taken out of them? Over and over and over. How come I end up with a dad that'd rather spend his time in the pub than at home? But the thought that keeps coming back, the one that won't go away, is: *I don't want to be here, I don't want this to be happening, I want it to end.*

Maybe this is what it was like for Henry, before he done himself in. Was that why he blew his brains out? Cos he couldn't stand it any more? Cos he couldn't go on for another day feeling like this? Cos he just couldn't face waking up the next day feeling the same way?

The tears have stopped now. I feel angry. At everyone. But I'm angry at myself more than any of them. Cos it's all down to me, the reason that this stuff happened. I must be like a magnet or something, attracting all this hassle. Like a shoe that can't help but land in shit with every step. That's me. And if I don't do something about it, it's gonna keep happening for the rest of my life. I open my eyes, wipe them on the sleeve of Zoë's jumper. It doesn't smell like her any more. It smells of tractors and gun oil and BO. It smells nasty. It smells like me.

I sigh, and look around the field. I think back to when I was seven or eight, back to when Henry was alive, when there were cows in the fields, when Dad worked here and I helped him. Why can't it be like that again? With Dad giving a shit about me, instead of spending all his time in the Swan getting pissed up. That's what I want. That's what I *really* want. More than anything in the world. It isn't gonna be like that again, though. Never. Henry's gone. The farm's gone. And Dad might as well have gone. It's over. Things are rubbish. And that's the way they're gonna stay.

I pick up the gun by the barrel, rest it on my shoulder, look down the barrel and take aim at a rusty tractor in the field. My finger's resting on the trigger. One movement, one second and I could fill the tractor full of lead. I sigh. I put the gun down, let it rest in my lap. When Henry shot himself, he stuck his bloody gun in his mouth. Pulled the trigger. Covered the walls in farmer brains. Just like that. BANG. One second he had all this shit going through his head, the next just a load of shot. And then nothing . . .

I take a few deep breaths. I can feel the tears coming back. I screw up my face and I start sobbing again. I just can't stop myself. So I pick up the gun. Turn it, so the barrel's facing me. I open my mouth. The metal of the barrel clunks against my teeth. Makes me cringe. Makes me feel sick. I close my eyes, put my finger on the trigger. One pull and it's over. No more Gary Wood. Then I don't have to think these stupid thoughts any more, don't have to feel like this. I squeeze my finger against the trigger. One more movement. That's all it'll take. One more squeeze and . . .

But I can't do it. I take the barrel out of my mouth. And tears start to fall down my face again. I can't even kill myself properly. I pick up the gun, aim at the rusty tractor again and squeeze the trigger.

BANG.

I smack into the wall of the barn as the shot flies out of the end of the gun. Jesus. It hurts. My back hurts. I think it's bleeding. It stings like mad. Stupid idiot. I should have known it'd do that. What a dickhead. I shift myself forward a bit, away from the wall, and I reach around under my shirt. There's a graze there. It stings a bit when I touch it or when my shirt touches it. I put the gun down next to me on the grass and I get up. I walk over to the rusty tractor. It's an old Ford. It was full of rust holes anyway. But now it's full of holes where the shot hit it as well. Looks like all it needs is a good kick to finish it off for good.

I turn away from the tractor, look up at the sky. All the clouds are blowing over. Most of the sky's blue now. I can feel the heat of the sun on my back. I think about taking my jumper – Zoë's jumper – off. I'm too hot in it. But I don't want to take it off. I want to keep it close to me. I want her to be here now. If she was here, she'd be telling me to stop feeling sorry for myself. She'd be saying that nothing's as bad as you think. But she doesn't know what it feels like to be me, to be inside my head. She doesn't know what it's like to have a head so full of . . . of . . . of I don't know what, but so full that you just want to find the 'off' button and switch your brain off. But maybe she'll never see me again. She probably wouldn't want to, either, after what I did yesterday, after what I did this morning. She must realise by now that I'm bad news, just like everyone else has.

I walk over to the farmhouse. The tape that the police put up around it has started to come away. Some of it's flapping in the breeze. I go to the window, put my face right up to the glass and shade it with my hands. I look at the table. Where Dad found Henry. Where Henry sat down when he'd finally had enough. Where he ended it all. You wouldn't think it now, looking in there. They cleaned it all up. One day someone will buy this bloody farmhouse, if they don't knock it down. One day someone will have a table right there, near the window, where they'll eat their breakfast and look out across the fields. And no one will ever tell them that where they're sitting is where someone put a shotgun in their mouth and pulled the trigger. Cos no one would buy the house if they knew that.

I turn away from the farmhouse and start walking back across the field. I put my hands into the pocket at the front of Zoë's jumper. I feel the pot of bubble mixture, the one she bought in East Strand. I smile. Just for a second. And then I take my hands out of the jumper and I walk through the gate.

Zoë

Today has gone so slowly. And all day I've had only one thought: *I need to get home. I need to find Gary. I need to know that he's all right. I need to tell him what's happened. That everything isn't as bad as he thinks it is.*

When the bus finally puts us down in Wallingham, I rush straight off. There's only one place that I can think of to look. Henry's farm. If he's not there, then I don't know where else he could be. I race right through the village, running down the roads, past my road and out of the other side of the village, towards the farm. And as I walk up the road, past the hedges that shield Henry's field from view, I feel nervous.

About whether he's there. About whether he wants to talk to me, whether he even wants to listen to me. About whether he's still alive.

As I get close to the gate, I see something up in the air in front of me, drifting across the road, glinting in the sunshine. Bubbles. Loads of them, being carried up and away by the wind. I run the last few metres. And there he is. Gary. Sitting on the gate that he drove through yesterday, the bubble blower near his mouth. He looks up at me as I walk towards him. He takes the bubble blower away from his mouth and looks embarrassed. I smile at him. He just looks back at me.

'Gary.' I don't know what else to say.

He doesn't answer. He just looks back at me, like there's something that's confusing him.

I walk up to him, climb the gate and sit up there too. The gate creaks a bit, like it'll buckle under our weight, but it holds steady. 'Are you OK, Gary?' I say.

He puts the bubbles away, in the front pocket of my hoodie. He shrugs. 'Not really.'

'Have you been home?'

Gary shakes his head. 'No.' He looks down at his feet as he swings them out in front of him.

'You should,' I say.

Gary looks up, not at me, but across the road, at another field. 'Why's that?' he says. 'So I can get in trouble? So my dad can give me a slap for not coming home? So they can send me to see a shrink? So the police can nick me? I've messed everything up, Zoë.'

'They're worried about you, Gary. They want you to come home. They'll probably report you missing if you don't go home soon. And then the police'll be looking for you.'

Gary doesn't say anything.

And I don't know what to say. Or at least I do – I have about a million things that I need to say to him – but I don't know how to start. So I just open my mouth, without thinking, and blurt something out. 'I saw you at school this morning.'

Gary turns slowly. He looks at me for a second and then looks away again. His cheeks are red.

'It was a stupid thing to do, you know, Gary,' I say.

He looks down at his feet again. 'I know,' he mumbles.

'It was funny, though,' I say. 'Sort of.'

Gary looks up at me. He looks confused again. 'It wasn't,' he says quietly. 'It was a psycho thing to do. They'll lock me up if they find me. I made him think he was gonna die.'

I look away for a second. He's right. I just wanted to make him feel better.

'Did he go and tell Mr Moore?' Gary says.

I nod. 'Yeah.'

Gary laughs. 'Well, that's me fucked, then! I'll be

chucked out for good,' he says, almost like he's relieved.

I don't say anything for a few seconds. I just listen to the wind blowing across the field, listen to the birds calling. But it's too much. I have to say something. 'Paul Knaggs has been given an exclusion,' I say as casually as I can.

Gary's head spins round. But he doesn't say anything right away – he just looks at me, with his mouth wide open. The wind ruffles his hair.

I smile at him. 'I'm serious,' I say.

Gary keeps staring. 'Why?'

'Because of all the stuff he's done,' I say.

'But –' Gary starts and then stops.

'It was David,' I say. 'He felt bad about what happened. He came and found me, made me go with him to see Mr Moore. We told him the whole lot.'

Gary looks away from me, at the ground. He's got this weird look on his face. I can't tell if he's happy or sad or what.

'Are you all right?'

Gary nods his head. He slips down off the gate. He looks dazed, like he doesn't know what's going on.

'Mr Moore's not gonna throw you out, Gary,' I say. 'He said so. He just wants to talk to you.'

Gary looks at me again. No smile. No thank you. Not that I thought there would be. Then he looks away again. 'I'm sorry, Zoë,' he says. 'For everything.' And he takes off my hoodie. He hands it to me. 'I'm going home,' he says. 'I'll see you tomorrow?'

I smile at him and nod. But he's already marching off down the road.

David

Mum and Ollie are already home when I get back. I can hear Ollie's music blaring out of his window before I even put my key in the door. And Mum's in the kitchen, sitting at the table with a cup of tea in her hands.

'Hi, David,' she says. 'Good day? Do you want a cup of tea?'

I shake my head, put my bag down and head over to the sink. I fill a glass up with water and take a gulp. And then I go back to the table. 'You all right, Mum?'

She looks up at me with a start. 'What? Sorry, David. I'm OK,' she says in this really flat voice.

I stare back at her. I wish I hadn't asked. I don't know what to say to her now.

But it doesn't matter, cos Mum opens her mouth again and says, 'Margaret phoned earlier, David. Gary's still not been home.'

My stomach turns over. I look away from Mum. 'Oh,' I say. I think about telling her what happened at school today. But that'd probably just make things worse. Besides, she might know already if she's spoken to Gary's mum.

'Margaret's going to phone the police soon if he doesn't turn up.'

I sigh. I still feel useless. Mum and me both stare into space without saying anything. After a while, I grab my bag and walk upstairs.

I lie down on my bed and switch my mobile on. As soon as it starts up, the message tone goes. Before I can open the message, the tone goes again. Two new messages. Both from Knaggs. I open the first one: **I can't believe u. Some friend u r.** I open the next one: **Ur dead when I get back to school. No one likes a grass u know.**

I switch my phone off and throw it down on my bed. I shut my eyes. What a mess. Even when I decide to try and put things right, I leave it too late. Wood's probably done something stupid by now. He's probably got a real can of petrol and blown the school up. Jesus! I don't even want to think about what he's done. Cos it's partly my fault.

I open my eyes again. I reach down the bed and grab my phone, switch it back on. I start to write a reply to Knaggs: **I was only doing what was right. I'm sorry. Wood is still missing. I'm worried. I wish I knew where to find him.** But as soon as I've written that, I know I can never send it to Knaggs. There'd be no point. He wouldn't understand. So I switch off my phone instead. And I lie back down on my bed and concentrate on listening to the thump of the bass drum coming through the wall from Ollie's music, so I don't have to think about anything else.

A few minutes later, there's a knock at my door. I sit up. Mum comes in. She's got tears in her eyes. She comes and sits down on my bed. She wipes the tears away with her sleeve and looks at me. And I feel like I want to be sick. I don't ever want to hear what she's gonna say.

'Margaret's just phoned.'

Oh shit. I look down at the floor. My heart beats like mad. My temples feel like someone's pressing them with their thumbs.

'Gary's come home.'

Acknowledgements

I would like to thank all the staff on Bath Spa University's MA in Writing for Young People, where this novel was started. In particular I would like to thank Jonathan Neale for his excellent advice, encouragement and enthusiasm. I'd also like to thank Alex D., Alex H., Elen, Janine, Liz, Matt and Sue. Lastly, I would like to thank Emma and Caroline for the faith they have shown in me.